BY BRANDON SANDERSON

ALCATRAZ VS. THE EVIL LIBRARIANS

Alcatraz vs. the Evil Librarians
The Scrivener's Bones
The Knights of Crystallia
The Shattered Lens
The Dark Talent

With Janci Patterson

Bastille vs. the Evil Librarians

The Rithmatist

THE MISTBORN TRILOGY

Mistborn
The Well of Ascension
The Hero of Ages

THE RECKONERS

Steelheart
Firefight
Calamity

SKYWARD

Skyward
Starsight
Cytonic

With Janci Patterson

Skyward Flight:
The Collection

BY JANCI PATTERSON

A THOUSAND FACES

A Thousand Faces
A Million Shadows
A Billion Echoes

THE SKILLED
(With Megan Walker)

Sinking City
Drowning City
Rising City

BRANDON SANDERSON
and
JANCI PATTERSON

Illustrations by
HAYLEY LAZO

STARSCAPE

A Tom Doherty Associates Book * New York

Illustrations by Hayley Lazo

A Starscape Book
Published by Tom Doherty Associates
120 Broadway
New York, NY 10271

www.tor-forge.com

Library of Congress Cataloging-in-Publication Data

Names: Sanderson, Brandon, author. | Patterson, Janci, author. | Lazo, Hayley, illustrator.
Title: Bastille vs. the Evil Librarians / Brandon Sanderson and Janci Patterson ; illustrations by Hayley Lazo.
Description: First edition. | New York : Starscape, 2022. | Series: Alcatraz versus the Evil Librarians ; 6 | "A Tom Doherty Associates book"
Identifiers: LCCN 2022014525 (print) | LCCN 2022014526 (ebook) | ISBN 9781250811066 (hardcover) | ISBN 9781250811103 (ebook)
Subjects: CYAC: Fantasy. | Librarians—Fiction. | Humorous stories. | LCGFT: Fantasy fiction. | Humorous fiction. | Novels.
Classification: LCC PZ7.S19797 Bas 2022 (print) | LCC PZ7.S19797 (ebook) | DDC [Fic]—dc23
LC record available at https://lccn.loc.gov/2022014525
LC ebook record available at https://lccn.loc.gov/2022014526

Our books may be purchased in bulk for promotional, educational, or business use. Please contact your local bookseller or the Macmillan Corporate and Premium Sales Department at 1-800-221-7945, extension 5442, or by email at MacmillanSpecialMarkets@macmillan.com.

First Edition: 2022

Printed in the United States of America

0 9 8 7 6 5 4 3 2 1

For Cortana and Kenton,
who share their talents with me every day.
—JP

For my three boys, who inspire me each day.
—BS

For my parents, Tom and Margie,
who taught me how to imagine,
and supported me every step of the way.
—HML

Author's Foreword

Alcatraz is an idiot.

For those of you who read *The Dark Talent,* the fifth installment of his memoirs, I don't need to tell you this. I'd also like to apologize for the ending of that last book. Not because I think I'm at fault, but in the way you might apologize for your great-aunt Gertrude when she arrives at your birthday party having forgotten her pants.

Seriously, Alcatraz. How could you do that to your readers?

Also, go put on some pants.

I, Bastille, am writing this book in Alcatraz's place because he has abjectly refused to do it himself, even though I've begged and threatened him, his Lenses, and his potted plants. He assures me that nothing frightens him more than having to continue his autobiography past the moment when he stopped.

I'm trying not to take that personally.

In the Hushlands, this will be published as a work of fiction, under the pseudonyms of Brandon Sanderson and Janci Patterson, to hide it from the evil cult of Librarians that controls your access to information about the world. By now, you know that the real Brandon Sanderson is a writer of fantasy books so large and boring that even Hushlanders won't read them.

The real Janci Patterson is not only a writer of fantasy, but also of romance, which is the most ridiculously fantastical genre of them all. No self-respecting Librarian is going to look here for a biography exposing how their evil ways nearly ended the world as we know it. Besides, have you seen the things Janci writes? Books about shape-shifter spies and romances about people falling out of canoes. No Librarian can figure out how to catalog *that*. I commend you Hushlanders for finding this volume.

In the Free Kingdoms, this book will be published as what it is—a completely true account of what happened after the tragic events in the Highbrary. If you haven't read the previous books in this series, might I suggest starting with book one? Otherwise, this book is likely to make no sense at all. To all those who had to suffer while waiting for this volume, you have my deepest apologies, especially those of you who missed the note I snuck in at the end of book five. Particularly those of you who had the Hushlands version, where my note was buried behind a "reader's guide," or some other sort of Librarian nonsense.

A conspiracy, if ever I saw one.

Regardless, I am here to tell you that the things Alcatraz told you about himself in the previous volumes of these memoirs are true.

(I have been told by my editor that some people, demonstrating a complete inability to follow instructions, will *not* read all the previous volumes immediately before beginning this one. She says I'm expected to *catch you up* on the story so far. If this is you, be glad that my years of working with the Smedrys have blessed me with unending patience. Also be glad that you're too far away for me to hit you with my handbag. *Or are you?*)

A reminder for those of you who demonstrate a Smedry-like inability to follow directions: you readers in the Hushlands (places like Africa and Europe and the Americas) have your minds blinded by a cult of evil Librarians who seek to control you. Those of us in the more advanced Free Kingdoms (places like Nalhalla, Calabaza, and the Kingdom of the Revered Former Republic of the Thunder

Lizards of Dino Land) are at war with the Librarians, trying desperately to keep them from spreading their control over the whole Earth.

I was largely absent for the fifth volume of Alcatraz's memoirs, given that I was rendered unconscious during the big battle with the Librarians in the Free Kingdom of Mokia. In my absence, Alcatraz set out to stop his father from enacting his crazy scheme to give Smedry Talents to all the people in the world, Hushlander and Free Kingdomer alike, which would no doubt result in the destruction of us all.

Alcatraz and the other Smedrys infiltrated the Highbrary (known as the Library of Congress to you Hushlanders), and were stopped by Biblioden the Scrivener, who sacrificed Alcatraz's father, Attica, to create a bloodforged Lens. Biblioden planned to use that Lens to push power through the Worldspire, burning up all Free Kingdomers and leaving only the Librarians to complete their terrible hold on the world. Remember now? Are you *happy*?

Even if you didn't remember that, I trust you remember the things Alcatraz has told you about himself. Alcatraz is, as he has said, a liar. He is, in his own estimation, not a good person. He can be stoopid. (I feel more stoopid for having typed that. Thanks, Al.) He has, at times, been a

coward. He is, first and foremost, an idiot. Most frighten-
ingly, perhaps, he is my husband.

But you already know all these things, right? I'm writing
this volume so that you will know the final truth: Alcatraz
is also one more thing, the thing he fears more than all
the others.

Alcatraz Smedry is a hero.

I hope you'll forgive me, Al. But it's true.

Chapter

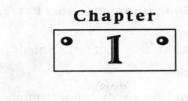

So there I was, in my pajamas, having a perfectly good nap, when the world decided to end.

I awoke to the distinct scent of cinnamon, and a sense of growing dread. I was strapped to a bed in a room I recognized from the *Penguinator*—the Smedry family's glass ship. Beneath the cinnamon was a faint burning smell, like someone had set a bakery on fire.

The last thing I remembered was throwing a teddy bear at a massive robot in the Free Kingdom of Mokia. I did not know why I, Bastille Vianitelle Dartmoor the Ninth, Princess of Nalhalla and Knight of Crystallia, would now be in a burning *Penguinator* in my pajamas. I had even less idea what the *Penguinator* would be doing in a burning bakery. But I knew it must have something to do with the Smedrys. Where there are Smedrys, there are Smedrys in trouble.

It was my job to keep them *out* of trouble, and there I was, lying in bed.

I sat straight up, finding my sword also strapped to the table next to me. I snatched it by its hilt and pulled it free, then used it to slice through my own restraints. I carried the sword with me as I ducked through the door and moved toward the hatch of the *Penguinator.* The hatch had been damaged in a crash, and I drew upon my Crystin strength. Power flowed through my Fleshstone—a crystal embedded in the back of my neck, which connected me to the Mindstone, and through it to all the Knights of Crystallia. I gave the hatch a mighty kick with my bare foot.

The hatch gave a resounding *clang,* and then fell open. I looked out into a wide cavern filled with small stone huts. The wreckage of the *Penguinator* was smoking a bit, but I wasn't in a bakery. I was somewhere far worse.

A *library.*

Not just *a* library, from the looks of it, but *the* library. An archive this vast could only be the Highbrary, beneath what the Hushlanders called Washington, DC.

At the center of the room was a tower, crowned by an

altar built out of massive stacks of outdated encyclopedias.

On that altar was strapped a thirteen-year-old boy
with messy, dark brown hair.

Alcatraz.

I didn't know what the Librarians were trying to do to
him, but whatever it was, I was going to stop it.

The Librarians must have anticipated this, because
every last one of them turned their guns on me and fired.

Only Librarians would come at me with such primitive weapons. I dodged, drawing on my Crystin powers
to lend me speed and precision as I used my sword to deflect some of the bullets back at the shooting Librarians,
who ducked for cover.

I leaped out of the doorway of the fallen *Penguinator*
and bobbed through the maze of huts. This room was
some kind of central chamber filled with many archive
buildings, some of which were overflowing with oddi-
ties like cards with strange symbols and small writing. (I
have since learned from Alcatraz that these were "Magic
cards," though there didn't seem to be anything magical
about them to me.)

The Librarians continued to shoot at me, and more
opened fire from up on the tower where they were holding

Alcatraz. I dashed between the buildings, my sword held out in front of me, and wove toward the central tower.

I got there just in time to see a Librarian partway up the peak loosening the bolts on the metal stairway that led up the side of the tower. One section tumbled down with a crash, and the Librarian moved on to the next one.

I reached for the Crystin power, pushing faster up the stairs, while the frightened Librarian tried frantically to loosen more of the stair bolts. When I made it to the missing section, I leaped and grabbed the lowest stair with my free hand, then hoisted myself up. I had barely climbed onto the step when a light flashed from the top of the tower, followed by a deafening, anguished scream. Another scream followed. It sounded like Alcatraz.

A pulsing metallic sound rang through the room as a Librarian airship, the kind with the big blades spinning atop it to hold it aloft, approached the peak.

It landed on the tower. They were going to take Alcatraz and Attica away with them; I had to stop them. I charged up the winding stairs and encountered another cluster of Librarians aiming their guns down at me.

They opened fire. I twisted, deflecting some of the bullets with my sword while dodging the rest, then launched myself into the air and landed right in front of the Librarians. They stumbled back, and I grabbed the one closest to the tower and punched him in the face, then shoved him into the others. The group of them fell from the stairs, leaving the pathway clear.

Footsteps pounded the stairs behind me, and I turned, whipping my sword up.

"It's just me!" Lord Kazan, Alcatraz's uncle, shouted. My mother, Draulin, was right behind him, looking like she wanted to leap over his head (Kaz was only four feet tall, so that was hardly a challenge even without the powers of the knighthood) to press on without him. They'd gotten past the gap in the stairs—to this day, Kaz won't tell me how he did it, but I suspect that my mother threw him.

Above us, the Librarian airship lifted off the tower.

Alcatraz. Without an airship of our own we wouldn't be able to follow, but I raced up the remaining stairs all the same. If I got there fast enough, maybe I could leap onto the airship. Maybe I could save him.

It turned out not to matter. We were too late, but not in the way I expected.

Alcatraz lay crumpled at the foot of the altar, leaning his head against an encyclopedia labeled x&y. Attica was still here too—

Or his body was—lying on the altar, broken and bloody, his heart removed from his chest.

"Alcatraz?" I said.

"Oh, Glass, no!" Kaz said, coming up behind me and moving toward Attica.

It was too late. We were *too late*. Alcatraz must have seen what they did to Attica, and—

"Kaz," my mother said, "we have to *go*."

At the time, I didn't know that Alcatraz's grandfather Leavenworth Smedry had pushed a self-destruct button. We did indeed have to go, as you will see very shortly.

At that moment though, I was more concerned with the terrible thing the Librarians had done to Attica. I was too late to stop it, but if the Librarians had escaped, we needed to know who they were and where they were going next. "Alcatraz, who was up here with you? A ship flew down and carried them off. Why did they leave you? Can you hear me?"

Alcatraz didn't respond.

"Pick him up, Bastille," my mother said. "With Leaven-worth and Attica dead, Alcatraz is now the last member of the direct Smedry line. We must get him to safety."

Leavenworth was *dead*? That couldn't be right. The old Smedry was like the wind or like . . . like birthday parties. The kinds of things you hate, but they sneak up on you anyway. Relentless and unavoidable.

I shook my head. Leavenworth was probably fine.

We'd escape and find him somewhere in his little tuxedo, chuckling to himself and wondering what took us all so long.

Kaz looked up at my mother, his mouth set in a grim line.

Shattering Glass, what happened here?

"They're scattering quickly," Kaz said. "I think the Librarian leaders must not have turned off the detonation that Pop set up. Why would they abandon so much? The Highbrary itself? And my brother . . . What is going *on* here?"

It didn't matter. My mother was right. Alcatraz was my responsibility. I'd failed him once—had it been only once?—and I wasn't going to do it again. I hefted him over my shoulder, turned my back on the altar of encyclopedias, and started to run down the stairs.

As I ran, Kaz's words started to sink in. "What did you mean, *detonation*?" I shouted over my shoulder.

"The library is going to self-destruct!" Kaz called, much closer than I expected him to be. When I glanced back, I found that my mother had lifted him onto her shoulders and was running along directly on my heels. "Pop triggered it to make the Librarians panic. He assumed they'd be able to turn it off, but maybe they chose not to."

That didn't make sense. The Highbrary was a Librarian holy site—they were trying to build another Alexandria. They wouldn't let all that be destroyed.

Unless they had a very good reason. I had a lot of questions, but this was not the time to ask them. Alcatraz, slung over my shoulder, groaned softly. He'd opened his eyes, but was staring sightlessly.

I'm sorry you had to see that, I thought. Attica hadn't been the best dad around, but he was Alcatraz's father all the same.

In the past, I'd seen Alcatraz smile and joke and complain and mope through situations I wasn't sure we would survive. The fact that he *wasn't* complaining or moping now was a testament to how bad things were. He'd watched Librarians butcher his father in front of his eyes. That does terrible things to a person.

So I didn't mind carrying him. I didn't expect him to simply snap out of this. Seeing something like that happen to someone you love, however complicated your relationship—it changes you.

But I hoped he'd be able to recover, for his sake.

We reached the gap in the stairs and I leaped over it, carrying Alcatraz with me. My mother landed behind me with a clang, and as I reached the bottom of the stairs she pulled ahead of me, Kaz still riding on her shoulders.

"What exactly is our plan?" I asked.

"Escape!" Kaz called back to me.

I had already gathered that much, though I don't know what else I was expecting. The Smedrys liked to bumble through things rather than plan them out.

I was hoping this might be something of an exception, mostly because I had no desire whatsoever to get blown up this early in a story. Explosions are terrible for your skin, and don't even *ask* what they do to your hair.

We ran between what felt like hundreds of little stone huts, all filled to the brim with junk. It was like the Librarians were a cult composed only of bargain-hunting grandmothers. The paths between the huts were also stone, and some curved high into the air, forming natural-looking bridges.

A few Librarians scampered across our path, wearing dark robes and clutching bottle caps, license plates, and cookbooks.

I swear, these grandmothers would catalog anything.

"There!" Kaz said, pointing to the hollow behind one of the stone staircases. Alcatraz's cousin Folsom Smedry was sheltered there, along with his new wife, Himalaya, and their team of reformed Librarians.

We approached them, and my mother stooped to allow Kaz to climb from her shoulders. I carried Alcatraz beneath the safety of the alcove as rocks tumbled down from the ceiling, smashing buildings.

My mother looked at Alcatraz and me with concern. You might think that was warranted given the circumstances, but this is my mother we're talking about. I can count the number of times she's looked at me with concern on one hand, even if I cut half the fingers off first.

Kaz scanned the ceiling for falling debris and then ran over to the wreckage of the *Penguinator*. We weren't going to be using *that* to get out of here, though maybe it would contain something useful.

I dropped Alcatraz, less than gently, and surveyed our situation. Some ropes led down from a large hole in the ceiling, but they'd all been cut short so the ends dangled dozens of feet up in the air—too high to reach.

I sighed. Looked like there was only one thing to do. "Lord Kazan," I called, "you should probably use your Talent to get us out of here."

Smedry Talents were something of a mixed bag— every member of the Smedry bloodline had their own unlikely and unpredictable power. I like things to be solid, trustworthy, repeatable. If not those things, then at least *stabbable*.

The Talents were none of those things. You could never tell what you were going to get when you engaged one. Kaz had a Talent for getting lost—so he could probably get us out of the Highbrary before it exploded. I didn't know where we'd end up, but virtually anywhere would be better than here.

Kaz pulled a briefcase out of the *Penguinator* and brushed off some fragments of glass. Then he looked back at me, wearily.

All the others were staring at me.

"What?" I demanded.

"The Talents don't work anymore," Himalaya said. "Alcatraz broke them."

"He broke *the Talents*?" Alcatraz's Talent is the most powerful and terrible of all: he breaks things. But to break the Talents themselves—how would that even work? "You're kidding me."

"Afraid not," Folsom said. "None of our Talents are functioning anymore. Haven't since the battle for Mokia."

I shouldn't have been so surprised. Leave Alcatraz with a bucket of purple paint, and you'd find him not only with a broken bucket, but with a pile of blue paint on one side and red paint on the other. He'd be covered in it too, most likely. Honestly, sometimes my charge to protect the Smedrys felt a lot like babysitting a bunch of three-year-olds.

I should probably have been happy. Smedrys without Talents should be like marginally less chaotic three-year-olds. But they were also less likely to get us out of here before the library exploded, so maybe they were *more* like three-year-olds, now that I thought about it.

"All right," my mother said, "what are our options?"

"Explode," Kaz said.

We all glared at him.

"What?" he said. "It *is* an option . . ."

I retreated farther beneath the stairs as another Librarian airship flew overhead. On second glance though, it looked like this one had been commandeered by a group of dinosaurs who were flying it in a zigzag pattern toward the hole in the ceiling. If they saw us, they didn't return to help us.

Useless dinosaurs.

"We need a vehicle," Folsom Smedry said. I've always thought of Folsom as one of the less annoying Smedrys. In the sense that one incessantly ringing alarm clock can be less annoying than another. Though I was going to miss his Talent for dancing really poorly, if the remaining Librarians stopped panicking about their bottle caps long enough to notice that we didn't belong here. I glanced at the shaking ceiling. "I don't know if we have time to go searching. This whole place seems like it's going to blow."

"No, no," Himalaya said. "It's not *that* kind of self-destruct mechanism. My former friends might be evil, but they wouldn't want to risk blowing up all the people in Washington, DC, when their Highbrary self-destructed."

"What, then?" I asked.

"Oh," the good Librarian said, "I suspect that the mechanism will fill this place with magma. We won't explode so much as *melt*."

Wonderful.

"So what do we do?" my mother asked as the cavern rumbled again. It *did* seem to be getting hotter in here. A group of Librarian minions ran past us, carrying armfuls of old receipts from a car wash. (Yes, they'll archive anything with words on it. No, I don't know what's wrong with them.)

"We can't escape," Kaz said. "So . . . maybe we can turn the blasted thing off? Over the radio, Pop said he'd turned on this self-destruct mechanism somewhere near where he'd found the controls to the ventilation system."

"Sounds like a plan to me," Folsom said. "And by that I mean, *AAAH! MAGMA! RUN!*"

He pointed at a distant part of the cavern, where red-hot magma had begun to pour in through a hole in the stone wall, bringing with it a wave of heat and the smoldering smell of brimstone. The magma splattered onto the floor and then flowed downhill in our direction.

Chapter

2

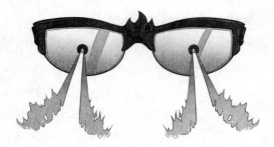

I've read all the other books in this autobiographical series, so I know how the chapters are supposed to start. Alcatraz says something obnoxious or condescending, or both. It's all part of Alcatraz's plan to present himself as a straw man—an irredeemable person without substance or integrity.

I have no desire to convince you I'm a straw man. Err, straw woman. I am *bursting* with substance, I will have you know. Plus I'm way too blunt to be condescending; if I think you're stupid, I'll tell you so, instead of implying it in some too-clever way involving forest animals and explosives. And for the record, I *don't* think you're stupid. After all, if you've survived this far reading Alcatraz's bizarre puns and obscure jokes, then you must be pretty darn smart.

Smart enough not to care about introductions when magma is about to kill everyone.

My mother, the good Librarian soldiers, and the gaggle of Smedrys all took off in a burst. I, of course, was left to heave Alcatraz over my shoulder and carry him again.

We ran in a jumble in the opposite direction of the magma—which, being magma, wasn't flowing terribly quickly. However, more and more holes were opening in the walls and letting the stuff pour out. I enjoyed imagining it falling on the heads of Librarians.

Himalaya took the lead. I hoped her sense of direction was better than her taste in men. I mean, marrying a Smedry? What kind of woman is *that* crazy?

Never mind. Don't answer that.

My trust in her proved to be well-placed as, even as she complained she didn't know her way around the Highbrary very well, she led us out of the main cavern and into a tunnel she said *might* lead toward a control room.

I was the last one out of the main chamber. I paused in the tunnel entrance and glanced back at the distant altar. I couldn't make out the corpse of Attica Smedry, but I could remember it. I shivered. I've seen a lot of disturbing things in my life. But that image of Attica still haunts me.

I'd failed. Yes, I'd been unconscious for most of what had happened here in the Highbrary, but I'm a Knight of Crystallia. I'm *sworn* to protect the Smedry family. We'd lost both Attica and Leavenworth, and ultimately, the responsibility for those losses rested on me.

(No, being in a coma is not an excuse. Because I said so, that's why.)

Magma consumed the base of the tower. Smoke rose throughout the chamber from archives set aflame. Heat made my brow prickle with sweat. I shook my head, bidding a final farewell to Attica Smedry—arrogant idiot though he was—and then ducked into the tunnel after the rest of the team.

The tunnel was typical Librarian fare. Blah blah skull-shaped lamps, blah blah dark ominous tunnel, blah blah we have no imagination. Unfortunately, the tunnel was *really* starting to feel hot. I risked a glance over my shoulder—the one *not* weighed down by an Alcatraz—and found that magma was seeping out of holes in the walls behind us.

Lovely.

Himalaya turned us through a metal door, which led into what looked like the Highbrary's clothing archive. Rack after rack was hung with shirts with text written across the front, pants with words written across the backside, and an entire wall of bins filled with those annoying tags that have to be removed from the inside of Hushlander shirt collars. (Why do you think the Librarians put those there, when literally any other location would be a more comfortable place for a tag to reside? It's because you're easier to control when you're uncomfortable, so they do their best to annoy you, one tiny clothing tag at a time.)

"I think it's through here," Himalaya said. "The way was labeled on a map I read earlier. The corridor has to be around here somewhere."

"Himalaya?" Kaz said. "As the expert in getting lost, I have to say, I don't think this is the way to the ventilation system."

Himalaya, Folsom, and the reformed Librarians wandered through the racks, trying to figure out the right way to go.

I set Alcatraz down and started browsing through the racks. "Bastille?" Kaz asked. "I don't think the way forward is going to be *between* the pairs of pants."

"No," I said. "But since I don't want to spend the rest of this book in my pajamas, I'm going to find something more becoming to wear."

Alcatraz, for whatever reason, had managed to be strapped to an altar of encyclopedias wearing a tuxedo. That didn't strike me as terribly practical. If I had to brave magma and murderous Librarians, I wanted protection, no matter how primitive. And as much as I would have loved a good set of Glassweave, I was limited to Hushlander clothing.

"Here!" I said, finally finding what I was looking for in a rack full of coveralls with various names written across the backs. I pulled down a hanger containing a full suit of black rubbery armor with one word across the back in white letters: POLICE.

Lice, for you readers in the Free Kingdoms, are tiny Hushlander bugs that like to burrow down in people's hair. The police, therefore, are the squads of Librarians tasked with detecting and removing such pests. They wear the armor to protect themselves from acquiring said lice.

I hid behind a bin filled with baseball caps plastered with various slogans and changed into my new suit of armor. It was a bit stiff—not nearly as flexible as Glassweave—and bulkier than I would have liked, but it would have to do for now.

I returned to retrieve Alcatraz, then hurried to catch up to Himalaya, my mother, and the others. Himalaya and

one of the other Librarians had paused to alphabetize a rack filled with bodysuits for infants, each of which had a saying across the front that I assumed served as hazard warnings about the viciousness of babies.

"Are you organizing things?" I asked Himalaya. "I thought you were reformed."

"We are," Himalaya replied. "From evil. Not from alphabetizing. We're not *monsters*."

Being so close to a lot of Librarians—recovering or not—made my skin itch. Probably because Librarians are like rashes: extremely irritating and likely to show up in unexpected places.

"I think I found something," Folsom called, and we all hurried to catch up with him, Alcatraz bumping along over my now-armored shoulder.

Folsom stood in a narrow corridor in front of another metal door. When he pulled it open, a red light on the wall started glowing, and a siren began to blare with a piercing sound. So I pulled out my sword and prepared to stab it. That does a pretty good job of shutting up people, after all.

"No, wait!" Himalaya said, and hit a button on the wall, turning off the alarm—though the light kept blinking red.

Drat. I lowered my sword. People often underestimate the value of a good stabbing.

This room was sleek, with metal surfaces and computer screens, like someone had tried to make it seem modern. Didn't fool me. The glass technology we had in the Free Kingdoms was *way* more advanced than this stuff. As the Smedrys clustered around the control panels, I set Alcatraz down and leaned against the wall, trying to cover up how tired I was starting to feel. It wasn't Alcatraz so much as . . . well, *everything.*

My mother walked up to me. "Knight Bastille," she said in her insufferably formal way, "do you require assistance?"

Shattering Glass. She had that concerned look going again. "No, I'm fine," I said. "I've only woken up from a coma to find myself needing to fight through three dozen Librarians, climb to the top of an enormous tower, heave a person over my shoulder, and run all the way to this room with barely a rest. I have no idea why you'd think I'd need assistance."

The concerned look turned into a disapproving glare, which felt much more comfortable. "Your testiness is unbecoming for one of your station, Knight Bastille. One might begin to worry that the Smedrys are rubbing off on you."

"No," I said, glancing at the catatonic Alcatraz, "but I do think one has been *drooling* on me."

My mother's look of disapproval deepened.

"This is bad, Bastille," she said. "We usually rely on the Talents to get us out of situations like these." She glanced out the door. The tunnel was glowing red from the light of the approaching magma, though none had reached our room yet.

I swallowed. "Lenses, maybe?"

Mother looked back at me. "Leavenworth is dead, child," she said, her face pale. "I saw him get shot by Biblioden himself."

Wait. *What?*

"He was shot by *the Scrivener* Biblioden? Leader and founder of the Librarians? A guy who is totally supposed to be *dead*?"

Mother nodded.

"Shattering Glass," I whispered. The old Smedry had been shot before, but he'd arrived late to the bullet.

He'd had a Talent then. I looked down at Alcatraz. His eyes were closed, though I wasn't sure if he was sleeping or simply trying to shut the world out.

His grandfather had been without a Talent, and that was Alcatraz's doing.

I could only imagine what kind of pain he was feeling.

"Was Biblioden the one who flew away in the airship, then?" I asked. "Was Shasta with him?"

"That was him," my mother said. "His cultists took Alcatraz's mother prisoner, but I don't think she left with him. I don't know where Shasta is now. I'm much more concerned about our own escape." She looked around at the others. "We have no Talents and no Oculators. Two heirs of the Smedry line dead, and one catatonic." She hesitated. "You did well, daughter. I want you to know that."

My mother was *complimenting* me. Worse, neither of us had done well, which meant she was saying that to make me *feel* better.

Things were really, *really* bad.

I knelt down beside Alcatraz. When I'd first picked him up, he'd looked somewhat awake and aware. But now he'd closed his eyes, and barely seemed to be breathing. He'd lost both his father and his grandfather today. He had every right to stare into the abyss.

This wasn't the way it was supposed to be. It shouldn't be surprising—with Smedrys around, *everything* tended to go wrong. But then they went right again soon after. People didn't end up dead on top of altars.

"Alcatraz," I said. "We need you."

He didn't so much as move. His brows were still drawn together, leaving little creases on his forehead, and my heart squeezed with sympathy.

(And, I'll have you know, *only* sympathy. I may be married to Alcatraz now, but at the time I regarded him purely platonically, as you will see from this entirely true account of the events that follow.)

"We need a miracle," I whispered. "Like you've always done before. I need you to be gregarious, to be foolhardy, to win when you shouldn't. That's what you do. Please."

In that moment, Alcatraz finally did something.

He started snoring.

Chapter

3

Those of you who found my note at the end of the previous volume of Alcatraz's autobiography (I congratulate you on your keen powers of observation) are probably wondering why I'm spending so much time on the mourning of Leavenworth Smedry. You know, after all, that old Leavenworth is not dead.

I would like to remind you that you only know about that because I told you, and I only knew long after this point in the story. At *this* time, we were all overcome with grief and guilt, both terrible emotions that, like kittens, tend to dig in their nails and bleed you dry one tiny drop at a time.

The disbelief I was feeling at the loss of Leavenworth was not at all like the disbelief *you* are now feeling. You are hopefully looking forward to the moment when it will be revealed to us that the grief was unnecessary, which spares *you*, the reader, the trouble of truly experiencing our pain. We, living through it, had no such relief.

You're welcome.

I left Alcatraz drooling on the floor and ran to Kaz, Himalaya, and Folsom by the control panels. They were arguing with several of Himalaya's freedom fighter Librarians—there were about two dozen of them, most watching out the doorway and muttering about the magma.

"Someone's *got* to know!" Himalaya said.

"Not me," said a broad-chested Librarian. "I mean, I figured Timpanogos would know."

"Not a chance," said a Librarian woman. "You think *I* actually read that thing?"

"That magma's very close, smart people," I snapped at them. "Hurry up and save us!"

"We're trying," Himalaya said. "But there's a password to deactivate the self-destruct mechanism!" She gestured at the screen.

It read, *Ulysses, episode 7.*

"A show?" I asked.

"It's a book," Folsom said. "By James Joyce. Widely recognized as one of the most important, thought-provoking, and challenging literary works ever penned."

"And so . . ." I said.

"None of us have read it," Himalaya admitted.

"But you just said it was important!" I exclaimed. "And challenging and . . . that kind of thing!"

"Well, yes," a Librarian said. "I mean, we all *pretend* to know about it for those reasons. But the truth is . . . well, when someone tells you a book is *important,* does that really make you want to read it?"

"I was meaning to," Folsom said.

"Definitely on my list," Himalaya agreed.

"I hear it's very profound," the big Librarian said. "That the literary allusions are quite brilliant."

"I've attended six lectures on it," the female Librarian said. "I mean . . . I'm sure that *one* of the lecturers read it."

"I fell asleep reading the summary," Folsom admitted.

"Ah, a *very* important book indeed," the big Librarian said, "if even the summary can knock you out."

"I know!" Folsom said.

I looked up at the screen, which—beneath the password request—was counting down a series of numbers. *The amount of time until this whole place is filled with magma,* I figured. *Only a few minutes left.*

Time for desperate measures. And by "desperate,"

I mean basically the same measures I always use. I lifted my sword, preparing to ram it into the control panel.

"Bastille!" Himalaya cried.

"What?" I said. "You don't know the password, and you aren't going to figure it out in time, right?"

"Well, that is true."

"So we should try to break the thing and see if it works." I shrugged. "What harm can it do?"

"Lots," Himalaya said. "No stabbing."

Such ignorance. I sighed, then glanced toward the corridor. The magma had reached us and was causing the bottom of the metal door to melt in little smoky bursts, seeping under it and sending a powerful wave of heat over us. (Some of you Hushlanders might point out that magma is only called magma when it's still in the earth, and so the flowing molten rock we were surrounded with might more accurately be called *lava*. I'd like to point out that you were taught that by Librarians. So there.) We were practically trapped in this room.

This was it, then. I'd failed the Smedrys, and now I was going to fail everyone else. The Librarians started arguing again, and I tore my eyes from the magma to look up at the large wall screens. Stupid ancient technology and its . . .

"What's that?" I asked, pointing at a screen. It displayed a drawing of several enormous fans inside metal casings.

"The ventilation system," Himalaya said. "We were thinking we could use it to cool off the magma in some way, but old Smedry locked out the central controls. The fans can only be controlled locally now."

"If there are fans," I said, "there has to be some way that they're drawing air from the outside."

"There is," Himalaya said. "But the shafts go straight up to the surface. There's no way we could climb them."

Maybe not, but I had another idea. "Where's the nearest one?" I asked.

"Just a little farther down the— Hey!"

She said that last part as I dashed away from the control panel and hauled Alcatraz up and over my shoulder. "Follow me!" I cried, stepping up to the door. The magma was collecting at the bottom of the doorframe, the heat overpowering. So I used my sword to cut the hinges off the door and kicked it down over a section of magma.

It immediately started to heat up, the edges melting and the resulting noxious smoke burning my lungs. I planted one foot in the center of the door and leaped toward a section of the tunnel beyond the closest magma vent, where the floor was still clear. Sweat dripped from

my forehead and I could feel the ends of my hair beginning to singe as I flew through the air, but I was able to
cross to a safe portion of the tunnel. The way back to the
main cavern glowed with a carpet of red molten rock.

The others huddled timidly in the doorway.

"Either cross that bridge before it melts entirely,"
I yelled at them, "or wait for the magma to melt you
inside!"

I started down the corridor as, one at a time, the others crossed the quickly heating door to join me. I reached
out a hand to catch them as they jumped across, avoiding
the magma. Everyone made it, fortunately, though the
big Librarian lost the lower half of his pants and melted
the soles of his shoes. We picked up speed, fleeing the
molten advance.

Kaz ran beside me, occasionally glancing over his
shoulder. "At least the stuff isn't moving quickly."

"Yeah," I said, trying not to show how exhausted I was.
Even having a Crystin stone in my neck didn't make me
able to go forever, unfortunately.

"Of course," Kaz added, "the magma itself isn't going
to be what kills us. It will be the smoke and the heat. That
will lay us flat long before we get burned by the actual
rock."

Such a delightful conversation. His words made me

keenly aware of how much I was sweating, and how alarmingly hot the tunnel was becoming. As we traveled farther down it though, the air grew cooler, and a breeze gained strength. We were approaching the fans. Indeed, we soon reached a place where the tunnel ended in an enormous pit. A fragile-looking bridge extended over the hole in the ground, swinging in the powerful wind being pulled down by the fans.

A group of Librarians had just finished crossing the bridge. One pointed back at us. Another pulled out a large axe. (P231 BackBreaker, looked like the 2001 edition, with optional balancing spike and faux-sharkskin grip. Not a bad weapon, but I'm more a P241-type girl.) She then proceeded to cut down the bridge and laugh maniacally, before joining the rest of the Librarians in fleeing farther down the tunnel on the other side.

"Those monsters!" Folsom cried. "Now we're trapped!"

I wasn't paying much attention. I leaned over the edge, looking down at the large fans below. I couldn't make out many details; there wasn't much light.

"Maybe the wind will slow the magma," Himalaya said hopefully, looking to her Librarian rebels.

Doubtful. I was surprised the fans had worked this long, honestly. They'd probably go out as soon as the Highbrary's power source succumbed to the heat.

My mother was watching me with a curious look. I took a deep breath. "Here," I said, tossing Alcatraz to her. "Hold my luggage."

And then I dove off the ledge into the pit.

I thrust my sword in front of myself as I fell, pointing it directly between the blades of one of the fans, hoping and praying that my aim was on. I hit sword first, and was rewarded with a metallic grinding sound and a *jolt*. When everything stopped shaking, I found myself holding to the hilt of my sword, my feet planted on the frame of one fan, while the enormous blades below me made a loud whining sound and strained to move. The sword, however, was lodged in place between the fan blade and the steel support girders that ran just above it and beneath it.

Excellent. I let out my breath. Step one of my plan—not getting chopped to pieces—seemed to have worked. So far. The machine continued to strain. My sword was made of strong stuff, but I figured it was best not to push things. I let go of the hilt of my sword and moved across the frame at the edge of the fan to the wall of the pit, fully aware that my weapon could slip out of its place at any moment, causing the blades to start spinning again. If the wind pushed me off balance, I'd quickly become a Bastille smoothie.

"Bastille?" Kaz called from above. "Uh, I know that being melted by magma isn't a particularly *noble* death, but don't you think jumping to your death was a bit of an overreaction?"

"I wasn't jumping to my death," I growled, pulling open a hatch on the wall and revealing a set of manual override controls for the fans.

This next part was going to be tricky, but since this was a library, the switches were nicely labeled. I threw a few switches, then dashed back along the girder, snatching up my sword as all of the fans powered down and then slowly started to move again. I shouted and threw myself into the air toward the wall, ramming my blade into the steel and then hanging there, feet pulled up, as the fans powered up again.

But this time, the blades were spinning in the other direction.

"Get ready!" I shouted up toward the others. "I turned off the safety switch that kept the fans from going too fast!"

Beneath me, the fan spun faster and faster, its blades becoming a blur inches from my feet.

"Why?" Kaz called down.

"Because," I shouted against the roar of the wind and the racket of the fans, "all this air has to go somewhere!"

The wind started to lift me upward.

Here we go . . .

I counted to three, then pulled my sword from the wall and spread my arms out. The fan churned beneath me, the air pushing against my body armor. I didn't fall. Instead I hovered there for a short time before starting to rise.

I went slowly at first. Then faster. By the time I passed the others on the ledge above, I was moving at quite the clip. I got one glimpse of them together, the magma almost reaching them, before I was blown into a large shaft in the ceiling.

"Follow Bastille!" I heard my mother shout.

In the blackness of the shaft, with the wind buffeting me onward, I almost forgot how high up I was flying. It was alarmingly hard to breathe in there, despite the wind all around me. I spent the trip worrying that the fans would overheat, and we'd all end up tumbling down to our deaths.

Light appeared up ahead. I rushed toward it, feeling a thrill of victory. I'd done it! We were free, and—

And . . . was that an ironwork grille over the opening? One I was traveling toward at roughly a hundred miles an hour?

As our dear friend Alcatraz would say: *Oh, grate.*

I swung my sword in desperation right before I smashed into the grate, slicing the bolts out of one side, so the thing flew open like a trapdoor.

The wind blew it backward before me, and I burst out into the sunlight of a small green park. A confused-looking man in a bow tie and trench coat stood beside the hole, and he watched me fly out into the air, arc over a swath of neatly manicured lawn, and then land with a thump right into a patch of mud.

Wait. Alcatraz always changed the details of these books to make himself look better, didn't he?

Well then, I flew up in a graceful arc and came down

to land like some kind of vampire chick from one of those action movies Alcatraz makes me watch: silver hair flaring, one knee down, one palm flat to the ground, and my sword pointed at the horizon and glimmering beautifully in the sun as it reflected my determined expression and smoldering-hot eyes. So there.

"Librarian scout?" I asked the guy in the trench coat.

"Uh, yeah," he said. "How did you—"

I laid him flat with one punch. (Librarians tend to be completely unable to take a punch. Comes from not having super-enhanced strength granted by a Crystin Fleshstone. Chumps.)

My mother shot out of the ventilation hole and landed in the mud. Unlike me. Totally unlike me.

Alcatraz, still snoring, came next. To my credit, I considered catching him, but then I decided the mud looked like a soft place to land. Not that I would know. And I certainly didn't decide to catch him and then miss, getting covered in mud when he went splat at my feet.

A torrent of Smedrys and former Librarians came next. After the last one, we did a quick count.

"All here," Himalaya said, lying back on the side of the hill. "I can't believe we survived that."

"I feel," Kaz groaned, "like a pinball."

(For you Free Kingdomers, a pinball is that little

ball that sits on the head of a pin. Kaz was referring to the upturned root he landed on, which pierced right through the seat of his pants.)

"It was a surprisingly effective plan," my mother said, standing up and brushing herself off. She was still wearing a Glassweave evening gown, and she had her sword strapped to her back. "It was, however, reckless not to inform the rest of us. Perhaps once we return to the Free Kingdoms, Knight Bastille, it would be better to assign you to duty far from the Smedry clan so that their influence can have time to . . . wear off."

Back to her stern old self, then. Now that we were safe, I probably wouldn't be getting any more compliments.

"Where are we?" Folsom asked, settling down by his wife.

The Librarians argued on that point. I climbed the grassy hill and surveyed our position. I didn't know this area very well, but I was pretty sure that place across the river was Washington, DC.

It wasn't burning at all. No smoke. No broken buildings. No signs of any attack whatsoever.

"They've put up a glass veil," Kaz said, joining me. "To prevent everyone outside from knowing what happened in there with the attack. What you're seeing is merely an illusion."

"That means they must have prevented everyone inside the city from escaping," I said. The poor people, trapped in a sudden war zone, caught between two forces they didn't know about, much less understand.

Kaz nodded, then glanced back at our muddy, exhausted crew.

My heart sank.

The people inside the city at least would have their memories altered, and return to the comfortable, predictable world they were accustomed to.

For us, there would be no such respite. Attica and Leavenworth were gone; my mother and I had failed to protect them.

We'd escaped from the Highbrary, but to what end?

"Kaz," I asked softly, "what are we going to do?"

"I don't know, Bastille. I . . ." The diminutive man took a deep breath, then straightened. "We're going to stop the Scrivener, that's what we're going to do."

"From doing what?" I asked. "What is his plan? Why did he kill your brother, then leave the Highbrary to burn? What is *going on*?"

Kaz shook his head, baffled, and looked toward my mother, who was climbing up to join us. She shook her head too.

"He's harnessed the power of the Incarna," a voice

whispered from below. "He's accessed it through my family line, and plans to use it to do something terrible."

Together my mother, Kaz, and I turned from the hilltop and looked down to the person still lying in the mud near the ventilation opening.

Alcatraz had awakened.

Chapter

4

If you remember, back when I first met Alcatraz, I was kind of a jerk to him. I mean, I'm a jerk to him now too, but out of fondness. I didn't even know him the first time I hit him with my handbag—which, looking back, I realize I'm lucky he didn't break.

Oh wait. He did. One hundred and twenty-two pages later.

The point is, I was grouchy at Alcatraz the day I met him. Mean, even. And yes, I'm not the warmest cinnamon roll in the pan, but I made an extra-special effort to be mean to him that day. Why?

The answer is simple. I wanted to *be* Alcatraz.

All my life, I'd wished to be an Oculator. Oculators, as far as I was concerned, were *awesome*. And yes, I realize my mother is a superstrong, superfast Knight of Crystallia with enhanced skills and an enormous crystal sword. As am I. I like being a Crystin.

But that path was definitely not my first choice. I learned everything there was to know about Lenses, but it made no difference.

Oculatory magic is genetic. You have to be born to it. I was never going to be an Oculator, no matter how hard I tried. But Alcatraz—he got to be one of the most powerful Oculators I've ever met, and until six months ago he didn't even know what one was.

You Hushlander readers are probably expecting that by the end of this story, I will become an Oculator. It was my aspiration in life, after all, and you are accustomed to fictional stories of people who achieve their wildest dreams, no matter how impossible.

I am here to tell you that I, Bastille of the future, am not an Oculator. Unlike your fictional narratives, real life has no shape, no predefined arc. It can't be changed to turn out the way we would have liked.

As Alcatraz illustrated in the last volume, if we don't like the ending, we don't get to simply write another.

I ran down the hillside and grabbed Alcatraz in a hug. I'll have you know that I'm quite good at hugging, despite what you might think. A hug is just a type of grappling move where you don't try to leave the other person dead.

Alcatraz suffered my embrace, but didn't say anything. When I pulled back, his eyes had a haunted look to them.

Behind us, Kaz asked Himalaya and her team to scout the area and make certain we were safe for the moment. Then he walked over to join us.

"What was that you said, Al?" Kaz asked. "About the Scrivener? He's *really* back?"

Alcatraz nodded, looking exhausted. "He's been with us for years, pretending to be cousin Dif. He killed the real Dif and took his place. We ourselves took him with us on our infiltration of the Highbrary. We trusted him."

"That's impossible!" Kaz said.

But, as you already know, it wasn't. "I remember Dif," I said. "Though I only met him once or twice."

"He fooled us," Alcatraz said. "He pretended to have a Talent for forgetting and making other people forget. It was the perfect one to pick, because he could simply pretend to forget anything he couldn't explain, and no one would question him."

"He must have spent *years* on that infiltration," Kaz said, sounding impressed—which made me want to punch him. That shattering Librarian had killed Alca-

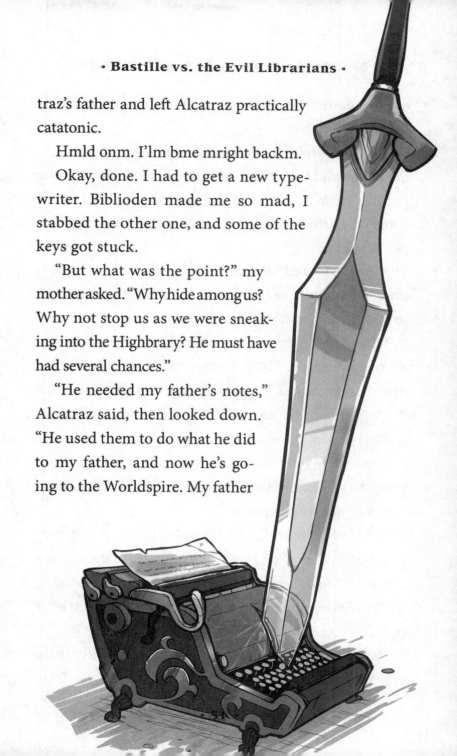

traz's father and left Alcatraz practically catatonic.

Hmld onm. I'lm bme mright backm.

Okay, done. I had to get a new typewriter. Biblioden made me so mad, I stabbed the other one, and some of the keys got stuck.

"But what was the point?" my mother asked. "Why hide among us? Why not stop us as we were sneaking into the Highbrary? He must have had several chances."

"He needed my father's notes," Alcatraz said, then looked down. "He used them to do what he did to my father, and now he's going to the Worldspire. My father discovered how to use it to affect all the people of the world."

The Worldspire, an enormous glass spike that juts out of the middle of what you Hushlanders know as the Pacific Ocean, is somehow connected to every human being on Earth. If you want to harm them all, that's the place to do it.

Alcatraz looked up at the sky with a morose expression. "It's because of me," he said. "Biblioden needed *me* to find my father. It's my fault. All of it."

I grabbed him by his bow tie and hauled him up into a sitting position. "No," I snapped. "No more zoning out." Besides, it was *my* fault. I was the one who decided it was a good idea to spend the entire last book in a shattering coma.

(You might be thinking that you'd like to tell me I'm being too hard on myself. I might be thinking about stabbing you with my sword.)

"My *father*, Bastille," he whispered. "They said they could take either of us, that it didn't matter to them. I was a coward. I *told them* to choose him."

The idea that it could have been Alcatraz on that altar instead of Attica . . .

Well, let's just say I may need another typewriter again very soon.

"You can't wish it had been you there instead of him," I snapped, still holding him by the bow tie. "What would that have accomplished?"

"You'd have him here, instead of me," Alcatraz whispered. "He'd know how to stop Biblioden. I'm useless to you."

"Hardly," I said. "You're *you*."

"I don't have a Talent anymore, Bastille. I'm nothing." He squeezed his eyes shut. "They shot Grandpa and killed my father. They've won. I failed."

He reached up to his bow tie and pulled on it so it came untied. It slipped off—leaving the tie in my hand—and he fell backward, eyes closed, to the grass. He refused to say anything further even when I prodded him. Or when I tickled his leg. Or when I poked him in the nose, stuck a blade of grass in his ear, put an ant on his forehead, pinched him on the pinkie finger, dropped mud on his eyelids, and kicked him on the bottom of his feet.

"Um, Bastille," Kaz said, "I don't think that's helping."

That was probably true. But it was keeping me from stabbing someone, which was a definite plus.

Kaz proffered the briefcase he took from the *Penguinator*. "This won't be much good without Alcatraz's help, but it's something."

I squinted at the briefcase. "What is it?"

"My father's case of backup Lenses. He left it behind in case he or Alcatraz lost theirs inside. Some are duplicates of Lenses he had with him. Others . . . I don't know."

I took the briefcase and knelt down on the ground beside Alcatraz. I was fairly certain he wasn't unconscious again. Maybe some new Lenses would get him to open his eyes and talk to us some more.

Inside the case, tucked into Glassweave pockets for protection, were four sets of Lenses. I pulled them out by the edges of their frames and inspected them.

The first was a pair of Windstormer's Lenses, offensive Lenses that blew a blast of air away from the face of the Oculator. Alcatraz had once used a pair in the Library of Alexandria in much the same way I used that fan—to propel us out of a pit. Next was a

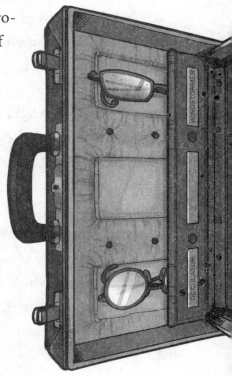

pair of Tracker's Lenses, which an Oculator could use to determine which way people went; the more familiar he or she was with the person, the longer the tracks would remain.

The third set had pale blue frames and a teal tint to them. I'd never seen them before, so I gathered they must be rare.

"Any chance you want to try these Lenses out and see what they do?" I asked Alcatraz.

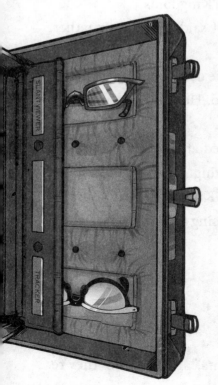

Alcatraz didn't respond.

I sighed and pulled out the last set—a pair of Oculator's Lenses. Those were basic, and only useful for sensing auras and otherwise noticing Oculatory activity. A good pair of basic Lenses, but they were not going to help us get to the spire and stop Biblioden—

From doing what now?

"Alcatraz," I said, shoving him a little. "What is Biblioden going to do at the Worldspire? Affecting all the people in the world with . . . what?"

At first, I thought he wasn't going to respond.

"The power of the Incarna," Alcatraz mumbled. "The thing that destroyed them. The Incarna filled themselves with magic, with raw energy, so much that they disappeared. Only the line of Alcatraz the First survived, because he figured out how to break the energy, how to give the Smedrys all the Talents to siphon it off. But Biblioden tapped into that power, took it from my father, and put it in a Lens. Now he's going to the Worldspire to distribute it to everyone in the Free Kingdoms."

"To give them all Talents," I said. "Like your father wanted."

"No," Alcatraz said. "To make us all burn up from the raw energy, like the Incarna did. He's going to make all Free Kingdomers cease to exist."

You may think I was alarmed at this news. That the revelation that Biblioden, having failed to take over Mokia and the rest of the Free Kingdoms, was going to burn us all up from the inside using the Worldspire filled me with fear.

I'm Bastille. I don't do fear.

Instead, I was angry.

No, incensed.

No, *livid*.

"And you broke the Talents," I said. "So they're

not siphoning off the power anymore, so not even the Smedrys will be safe."

Alcatraz nodded miserably and rolled over onto his side.

I wasn't sure what to do then. I could hold Alcatraz at swordpoint and tell him to try the Lenses so we'd have a better idea of what we had to work with. But with as thoroughly as he'd given up, I wasn't sure what good it would do. I wasn't willing to actually stab him. Not anywhere life-threatening, anyway.

I assure you that this was merely because he was our only remaining Oculator, and if I stabbed him the Lenses would be useless. Also because I was sworn to protect him, as a Smedry. And perhaps because I liked him a little. As a friend. I was not, I will remind you, attracted to Alcatraz at this point in my life, and was therefore totally not thinking about how much I missed his smile. I was also not thinking that said smile makes a person feel like they might be about to explode with the energy of the Incarna.

I couldn't have been thinking that, because at the time I didn't know what it felt like to be filled with the power of the Incarna. I did not yet know that it doesn't, in fact, make you explode.

It vaporizes you. There. Now you know what's going to happen at the end of this book.

What's that? You don't think I'm going to be vaporized? How would a vaporized person be writing this book, you say?

It's simple. I concentrate myself into a very dense cloud of vapor such that I can exert pressure on the keys one at a time. It makes . . . typing . . . very . . . slow.

You can doubt me, but you also doubted Alcatraz when he said the last volume would end the way that it did. And you were wrong about that, now weren't you? If you're so sure it doesn't happen, go ahead and turn to the last page of the book and find out if it's true.

Go on, I'll wait.

Told you.

No, while I was not ruminating on the effect of Alcatraz's smile, I was contemplating how to get him to snap out of his funk. If I had a horde of hungry kittens, that might do it. No, that would be too cruel even for me.

I sighed. I didn't *feel* like I was being filled with the power of the Incarna—which meant that Biblioden either hadn't reached the Worldspire yet, or whatever he was doing with that Lens wasn't an instant sort of process.

But wait. If the Smedrys had always been filled with the power of the Incarna, and had been using the Talents to siphon the power off . . .

"Alcatraz," I said, "if the Talents are gone, shouldn't you and the rest of your family be filling up with that energy right *now*? Before Biblioden does anything? If the Talents aren't siphoning off the power . . . where is it going?"

Alcatraz opened one eye and looked up at me. His eyes fell on the set of Oculator's Lenses, still in my hand, and he raised a single, solitary finger and tapped the Lenses at the edge of the frame.

The Lenses activated. That shouldn't have worked—Oculator's Lenses require you to be wearing them to function. I wouldn't be able to see anything through them of course, activated or not, but the Lenses seemed to vibrate with power—far, far more power than should have been possible.

The frames began to heat up in my hands.

I dropped the Lenses back in the case, but they kept heating up, slowly growing red around the edges. I was afraid they were about to melt.

Did all that power come from *inside* Alcatraz? He was our only Oculator, but that didn't matter much if everything he did with Lenses made them overreact like that.

"Alcatraz," I said, "can you turn it off?"

Alcatraz reached out and touched the Lenses one more time. His finger sizzled a little when he touched them, but the glow immediately began to fade as the Lenses cooled.

Then he shrugged and rolled away from me, as if there were nothing out of the ordinary.

This was worse than I thought. Even if we did stop Biblioden, was Alcatraz right? Were the Smedrys all going to die of excess power with no means to release it?

How had Alcatraz managed to break the Talents anyway?

I tucked the cooled Lenses into their protective pouch and closed the briefcase. Those four Lenses wouldn't be immediately helpful without an Oculator willing to use them. Besides—ha! "I'd ask you to put on the Lenses," I said, "but I wouldn't want you to end up with molten glass melted to your head. You might not be the handsomest guy around, but we wouldn't want you to end up *defaced*."

Alcatraz didn't move. He didn't smile. He didn't so much as twitch, though I did notice that he'd tucked his singed finger into his mouth, so that had probably hurt more than he let on. An Alcatraz who didn't react to puns was hardly an Alcatraz at all. He just stared straight ahead like a forlorn, tuxedoed traveler who hadn't seen a hairbrush in a week and felt forlorn about it. Forlornly.

(And I'm not even a writer. See, Alcatraz? It's not that hard.)

Clearly Alcatraz needed more time before returning to his usual plucky-yet-obnoxious self. In the meantime, the rest of us needed to carry on without his help.

"So," I said, "we need to get to the Worldspire."

"How do you intend to do that?" my mother asked. "There are Librarians crawling all over this area."

"I don't know," I said. "Most likely by doing something crazy and improbable that seems like it will never work but somehow does."

My mother raised her eyebrows at me. Whenever someone raises their eyebrows in a book, it means they are skeptical or surprised. Or sometimes it means that the author has run out of ways to describe things people are doing when they're standing still talking to each other, rather than doing something crazy like propelling themselves into the air using overclocked ventilation fans.

I'll let you guess which occasion this is.

"Knight Bastille," my mother said, "our first responsibility is to protect the Smedry line. Lord Alcatraz is the last living member of the direct line, so it is of the utmost importance that we find someplace safe to—"

"Do you think I don't know what our responsibility is?" I snapped. "Nowhere is safe. If we don't get to the Worldspire, Alcatraz will be snuffed from existence along with the rest of us!"

My mother glowered at me. (Hey! That's a good one. I should use that description more often.) "We are protectors," she said. "We don't go running off in the face of danger. You've been with that Smedry boy too long. He's a bad influence on you."

I glowered at my mother. This was about the time when I usually throw something pointy at the person who's telling me that I can't do anything about the mess we're in, but in this case that person was my mother, and I didn't think us having a full duel with Crystin blades with so many Librarians lurking around would be good for our cover.

My mother continued to glower at me. (What? She *did*. You try thinking of fifteen different ways to describe us staring at each other while we talk. It gets old.) "Bastille," she said, "you have four Talentless Smedrys, one of whom is an Oculator who won't think, move, or talk. How exactly do you propose we fight Biblioden? There's an entire continent and half an ocean between us and the Worldspire. We don't have a way to get there, let alone stop him."

I pressed my lips together. (But don't worry, I was

still also glowering at my mother.) "We can't just do *nothing*."

"Biblioden has an airship, Bastille," my mother said. "What do you propose we do to beat him there?"

I was quiet for a moment. Next to me, Kaz squirmed uncomfortably, probably because he was our usual means of transportation.

I've always resented the Talents for the effect they have on my life. In fact, I've always thought my dream life would look something like this:

My Happy Place

Man, wouldn't that be nice.

At that moment though, I felt kind of bad for Kaz. I remembered what it was like to be cut off from the Mindstone, the source of my power. It wasn't fun.

My mother and I were the only ones at full power on this mission, so that meant it was up to us to save the Smedrys. That was our shattering *job*. I had my Crystin powers. I had the will to help.

What I didn't have was any idea of how to go about it. Ideas are Alcatraz's department. Yelling at him for how stupid they are before they inevitably work—that's my contribution.

But I'd gotten us out of the Highbrary doing something that, while it had worked, was somewhat reckless in retrospect. If Alcatraz was too broken by what had happened to help, I could respect that. In the absence of both him and Leavenworth . . .

My mother was right. Alcatraz *was* a bad influence on me. Which meant I was our best chance at figuring out what to do next.

I hadn't responded to my mother, and by now she was looking at me with suspicion. (And yes, her eyebrows were raised. I mean, really. How many facial expressions do *you* use in a given conversation?)

"I'm thinking," I said, which I immediately realized was

my first mistake. A Smedry would not think. A Smedry, if he was not currently overburdened by the loss of some of his loved ones and of his ability to protect the rest, would simply *act*.

"We're going *that* way," I said, pointing to the bottom of the hill. And I marched off in that direction before anyone could argue.

Chapter

5

I lied to you in that last chapter. More than once actually, but right now I'm only willing to admit that I lied to you about how I type. Everyone knows that a vapor, being a gas, expands to fill its container, so the typing maneuver I described would be impossible.

What, you're expecting a fart joke here?

Please. I have a few things that Alcatraz doesn't have. Class, for example. Standards. Sophistication. And, finally, a *literary license.* Here, I'll show you. I got it from the book place down the street in Nalhalla. (I figured I should have one if I was going to write a book. Alcatraz, being a Smedry, was reckless enough to write all *five* of his books without a license. I expect him to be arrested any day now.)

LITERARY LICENSE

~~RODGERS~~ BASTILLE

BAGSWORTH BOOKS

WE ARE TOTALLY NOT AT ALL LIKE A LIBRARY, WE PROMISE

SHE CAME IN HERE WITH A SWORD DEMANDING WE GIVE HER A LITERARY LICENSE. PLEASE DON'T TELL HER IT'S NOT ONE. WE MADE HER PROMISE NOT TO READ THE BACK SIDE BY EXPLAINING THAT IT WOULD BREAK THE MAGIC, AND THEN SHE'D HAVE TO PAY FOR EACH VOWEL SHE USED UP.

That thing means I can write what I want in here, and I can do it the way I want. I can also *lie* if I want. (Remember when I told you I didn't think you were stupid?)

I took a few strides down the grassy incline before I turned around and discovered that Alcatraz was not following me. I could have continued to carry him, but now that he was conscious he could walk under his own power, which would leave me better able to punch and kick our way out of this situation if necessary. When he didn't follow me, I marched back up the hill, grabbed Alcatraz by the ear, hauled him to his feet, and dragged him after me.

Alcatraz woke up from his stupor enough to try to

wrench away from me while I held on to his ear cartilage and twisted in the direction I wanted him to walk.

"OW!" Alcatraz said. "OW OW OW OW OOOWWW OOOOOWWWWWWWWW!"

"Shut *up!*" I said, reaching the bottom of the hill and taking stock of my surroundings.

We were at the edge of what looked like some kind of small public park. The concrete lot below was mostly empty, except for the far side where a number of cars were parked next to one of the most horrifying sights I had ever seen.

There, next to the curb, with its back hatch open for business, was a bookmobile.

You Hushlanders are probably familiar with the traveling Librarian arsenals that invade your neighborhoods if they're deemed to be too far from a central Librarian control center. Free Kingdomers are probably less familiar: imagine a chariot full of weapons of misinformation prowling the streets of the Hushlands, complete with camouflaged snipers waiting on top, searching for dissidents.

I hauled Alcatraz down to the edge of the parking lot and behind a row of those big green metal dumpster things that Hushlanders use to house their chickens. (And never clean up after them, judging by the smell.)

"What are you doing?" Alcatraz shouted at me when I let go of his ear. "Are you trying to turn me into Van Gogh?"

"Keep your voice down," I snapped. "And what's a Van Go? Some kind of taxi service? Because yeah, that would be welcome right now."

Alcatraz looked at me like I was crazy. He's got a lot of practice at that. He's been doing it since the day we met.

My mother seemed to have spotted the bookmobile and alerted the others, because she moved down the hill with great skill and poise, joining us behind the dumpsters. Kaz stole frightened glances in its direction, but he moved as stealthily as a flatulent hippo eating a pile of potato chips.

Smedrys.

Folsom, Himalaya, and the reformed Librarians hadn't returned yet from scouting—and if they'd failed to find the bookmobile at the bottom of the hill, I wasn't convinced scouting was among their strengths. Or maybe they *had* seen the snipers, and were waiting to share this information until they could present an alphabetized list.

I took stock of our assets. My impulsive walk down the hill had (surprise!) not resulted in us finding transportation to the Worldspire, but grabbing Alcatraz by his ear *had* perked him up a bit. If I'd known how effective that would be, I would have started with it.

"Alcatraz," I said, holding up the briefcase, "there's a heavily armored Librarian assault vehicle nearby. It would be best if you had some kind of offensive Lenses for this. You need to try that last pair and see what they do."

"The bookmobile appears to be packing up," Kaz said. He peered out between the dumpsters in the direction of the Librarians. "Hopefully they'll leave without spotting us."

Alcatraz gave me a weary look, but he didn't lie down and try to go to sleep again, so I took that as agreement. I opened the briefcase and looked over the Oculator's Lenses, the Tracker's Lenses, and the Windstormer's Lenses to find the strange teal-tinted Lenses I didn't know the name of. "Here," I said to Alcatraz. "Put these on and tell me what they do."

Alcatraz reached for the Lenses immediately. More improvement. He held the Lenses by the very tips of the frames, and gingerly put them on his face.

He looked right at me. I wished he wouldn't, because if these Lenses did something awful, like steal the strength of the person he looked at, then we would be down one knight if it came to a battle with the Librarian agents.

Alcatraz looked down at his feet for a moment. The

glasses began to glow, but didn't seem to be melting his face immediately, so perhaps he wasn't going to explode from residual energy in the immediate future.

Alcatraz jumped and pulled off the glasses.

"What?" I asked. "Too hot?"

He set them down on the concrete in front of him. "No," he said. "I mean, they were starting to get warm, but . . . that was weird."

"Weird *how*?" I demanded.

"I was looking at you," Alcatraz said. "And then all of a sudden, I was looking at *me*. Like the glasses flipped around and looked at me, instead of me looking at everything else." He winced. "That doesn't make sense."

Ah. "Slantviewer's Lenses. I didn't know old Smedry had a pair. First you look at someone else to establish your target. Then you look at a subject, and you see it the way your target sees it."

Alcatraz scrunched his nose at me. He's kind of cute when he scrunches his nose, but don't tell him I said that. "So they let you see things from different angles? That doesn't seem very useful."

"That's because you lack imagination," I said. Though in this particular circumstance, I was inclined to agree with him. They weren't going to help us with that bookmobile.

I could see the Librarian crouched on top of the bookmobile now, a large firearm (Blenderbuss 3000 Exploding Edition) positioned in front of him. From inside the bookmobile I heard the rustle of paper.

"Oh no," I said. A large creature made entirely of old book pages emerged from the back of the book-mobile. It stood at least eight feet tall, huge and hulking. It was vaguely man-shaped, if that man had been shaped like a grizzly bear and had thick arms with little bits of rolled-up paper sticking out at odd angles. As it ambled toward us, every sheet of paper in its body rustled angrily.

This was an Alivened—an inanimate creature brought to life by dark Librarian magic. They liked to use old romance novels to do it. Something about the passion and emotion inside the books giving birth to the most horrible of monsters. They were dreadfully hard to kill. Alcatraz had done it once, with his Talent, during our first infiltration together.

I'd lost my sword during that fight. Granted, that had been Alcatraz's fault—most things are—but I wasn't eager for a repeat of the event. Especially now, when we had so few other resources at our disposal.

My mother moved to the end of the row of dumpsters to stand between Kaz and the oncoming Alivened, her sword held in front of her in a defensive stance. Kaz flattened himself against the side of a dumpster, looking like he wanted nothing more at that moment than to get lost.

I shoved Alcatraz back against the dumpster and stood in front of him. I might not have any great confidence that my sword could do much against an Alivened—there's a reason the Librarians like to use them to guard their libraries—but I was a Crystin, and I wasn't about to let one hurt him while I was still standing.

"Bastille," my mother said, "I will fight the creature. You and the others will run."

"I'm not going to run away and leave you here," I said.

"You will," my mother said, "because it is your duty as a knight to protect the Smedry family at all costs. They will need you to defend them from the sniper."

I could run away from the Librarian sniper just fine. But there was nothing nearby for us to run behind—Kaz and Alcatraz would have to take fire as they ran. I might be able to handle some of the bullets, but I couldn't be sure to deflect them completely. Normally, Kaz and Alcatraz had Talents to protect them from such primitive weaponry.

This time, however, they were sitting ducks.

(A sitting duck is a dodge performed while sitting. It's not very deft or effective, kind of like a Smedry.)

"Bastille?" Alcatraz said. "What kind of Lenses did you say were in that case?"

I would have taken some solace in the fact that he now *noticed* we were in danger—another improvement—if I hadn't been listening to the paper footsteps of the creature that was going to kill us all.

I mean, not that I was frightened. Clearly I wanted to trade blows with this fearsome creature and die in honorable battle.

Oh, who am I kidding? Sometimes, you're up against a threat that you know from experience you can't beat. At that point, running isn't cowardice. It's wisdom. And this particular battle was about to end the same way as a pun contest with a Gak.

(What? Gaks like to engage in wordplay. And at the end they eat you.)

"There were Oculator's Lenses, right?" Alcatraz said. "And Tracker's Lenses . . ."

"Plus Slantviewer's and Windstormer's Lenses," I said. "None that are offensive enough to fight an Alivened! Unless you want to get a fantastic view of its perspective while it murders you. Or do so with your hair blowing in the breeze."

Alcatraz put the Slantviewer's Lenses back in the case and reached for another pair. The Alivened—moving slowly and shaking its pages menacingly—reached the end of the dumpsters. Either we could stay here and get torn to pieces by the monster, or we could run and risk the lives of the non-Crystins against the Blenderbuss.

The Alivened turned the corner, its papery arms outstretched as it advanced on my mother.

"Bastille," my mother said, "protect the Smedrys. Go, now."

The Librarian atop the bookmobile opened fire. I shoved Alcatraz flat against the dumpster, using it as cover, but the bookmobile didn't seem to be firing at us. The Blenderbuss was aimed off to the side of the parking lot, in a direction where I could now hear the roar of one of those crude Hushlander motors and a whoop that sounded an awful lot like Folsom Smedry.

The dumpster at the end of the row lifted off the ground. Shattering Glass, was there a *second* Alivened attacking? The whoop continued, and the floating dumpster rammed straight into the bookmobile.

I blinked. An enormous truck with a fork on the front

had lifted the dumpster into the air. (The truck looked like it was *designed* for lifting dumpsters. Chickens in the Hushlands seem to have robust infrastructure for their own transportation. Good for them.) The truck was being driven by Himalaya, with Folsom riding in the passenger seat and the reformed Librarians clinging to the back.

"Coming through!" Folsom shouted, and I grabbed Alcatraz and rolled to the side. Kaz barely scrambled out of the way before Himalaya drove the truck, dumpster and all, straight at the Alivened. My mother leaped at the last moment, landing atop the dumpster and deflecting bullets from the Librarian atop the bookmobile.

"Bastille!" my mother shouted. "Get Alcatraz to safety!"

Alcatraz was still fumbling with the case of Lenses. The best way to protect Alcatraz right now was to stop that Librarian from shooting him. The bookmobile's driver pulled forward a bit, and then drove the bookmobile backward, straight at the dump truck. (Which is definitely what you call a truck that moves dumpsters. I mean, what else would you call it?)

I leaped into the air and landed on top of the moving bookmobile next to the Librarian sniper, then kicked his Blenderbuss away. It clattered to the ground, and the Librarian struck out at me. I slammed my foot into his stomach, propelling him off the moving vehicle.

I smiled. We were taking control of this situation.

At that moment, three more bookmobiles sped up the road and rumbled into the parking lot.

If they all had Alivened in them, we were in serious trouble.

Papers shivered behind me, and I turned to see that Himalaya had run down the Alivened, pushing it across the pavement. She had also evaded the blow from the oncoming bookmobile.

"Bastille!" Himalaya called, "Protect Alcatraz! We'll try to distract them!"

Alcatraz was standing stupidly behind one of the remaining dumpsters with a pair of Lenses in his hands. I didn't take the time to figure out which ones. I leaped from the top of the moving bookmobile and landed gracefully in front of him. I put up my sword, ready to deflect bullets from the oncoming bookmobiles. At least one of the new ones sped across the parking lot, ready to chase Himalaya and the others as they fled. Kaz had managed to climb onto the back of the truck with the reformed Librarians, and my mother was running along the top of the truck over to where she could protect them.

Only Alcatraz and I still needed to escape. The truck was too far away now—I couldn't simply leap onto it, especially with Alcatraz in tow.

"We're going to have to run for it," I said.

"I have another idea," Alcatraz said.

Oh, good. Ideas were definitely progress. "Well? What is it?"

"I'm sorry, Bastille."

"Shut up, Alcatraz!" I said. "Not everything is your fault!"

"I know," Alcatraz said. "But this is."

And then, without warning, he stepped between me and the oncoming vehicles. I was about to grab him by the shoulders and throw him out of the way, but he wrapped my arms around his shoulders, like he was preparing to give me a piggyback ride.

Then he put on the Windstormer's Lenses.

You may recall that Alcatraz once used a pair of Windstormer's Lenses to blow us out of a pit in the Library of Alexandria. Those were *ordinary* Windstormer's Lenses, powered by an average amount of Oculatory magic.

This time was entirely different. Alcatraz looked down at his feet and tapped the Lenses. A huge blast of wind shot from the Lenses, strong enough to slide the metal dumpsters across the concrete directly at the bookmobiles. I kept my arms wrapped around Alcatraz as we went flying up into the air.

It was definitely Alcatraz who screamed, not me.

Alcatraz was the one who stared down at the buildings below us rapidly turning into tiny dots and felt like he was going to pass out.

Totally Alcatraz.

Certainly not *me*.

For those of you keeping track at home, yes, I do hate heights. Yes, this was the second time that day I'd intentionally flown myself up into the air using an uncontrolled aircraft (first: myself, second: Alcatraz).

The previous time, however, had been up through a dark shaft, not out in the daylight where I could clearly see all the things below me that we were potentially going to land on when we fell out of the sky.

Up Alcatraz and I went, until the details of the things on the ground grew much less clear. I still gripped my sword in one hand, and Alcatraz had his arm through the handle of the case full of Lenses so it wouldn't fall. The Windstormer's Lenses didn't seem to have adhered themselves to Alcatraz's face yet, or at least he wasn't writhing and clawing at his face the way I'd expect him to if the Lenses started to burn.

Unless Alcatraz *had* passed out, either from the shock of flying up into the air at such a rapid speed, or from the way I was clinging to his neck, possibly strangling the life right out of him at that very moment.

By this time, we were so far above the Earth that we could see for miles up and down the coastline. If we didn't do something fast, we were going to go into orbit.

And how, you Hushlanders are saying, did I continue to breathe? Isn't the air in the upper atmosphere supposed to be thinner? Surely Alcatraz and I should have fainted from the changes in temperature, pressure, and oxygen concentration and then lost all control of where the Lenses were facing and plummeted to Earth, splatting across the pavement like a dropped ice cream cone.

This is because you believe in a thing called *physics,* which is a Librarian fabrication.

(Splatted ice cream cones, however, are real. All *too* real. *shudder*)

If Alcatraz wasn't going to steer us in any particular direction, I was going to need to reach up and grab Alcatraz by his windblown hair and twist his head opposite the direction we needed to go. We couldn't possibly do this all the way to the Worldspire, which was in the Pacific Ocean— you know, the one on the other side of the continent.

I loosened my grip just a little, and was nearly blown off of Alcatraz's shoulders as the wind rushed beneath us. I couldn't reach to turn his head, and I wasn't sure he would be able to hear me if I shouted. So we were going to go up and up and up and up, until—

Alcatraz turned his head.

It was subtle, a slight lift of his chin, with his face still mostly aimed down at the ground. But we began to soar over Virginia, the wind pushing us upward at an angle, Alcatraz's face aimed toward the ground and our feet up above, buffeted by the air that we were rapidly cutting through.

I squeezed my eyes shut. If Alcatraz had the directions covered for now, I was going to pretend I was somewhere else. Somewhere very, very windy where I was hanging face-first at a forty-five-degree angle to the ground for some reason.

A wind tunnel? Yeah, that is not my happy place. Let me remind you what my happy place looks like.

My Happy Place

As I squeezed my eyes shut, trying to imagine that I was reading a book outside a cage full of Smedrys *atop an enormous ventilation fan,* I felt Alcatraz pull on my hands. I could tell—if only by the vibrations in his throat, which I'll remind you I had in a death grip to keep from falling miles out of the sky—that Alcatraz was trying to say something. Rather than loosen up and risk falling, I pulled myself closer, moving my ear up alongside his face.

Ouch. The frames of his glasses were hot—not hot enough to melt his face off yet, but hot enough to be uncomfortable.

In fact, that's what Alcatraz was shouting. "Hot! Have to turn them off!"

I pressed my mouth into Alcatraz's ear. This gesture, even miles up in the sky, and despite my fear for the integrity of my body parts if we fell, made my neck feel hot.

"No, you idiot!" I shouted. "If you do, we'll fall!"

Now, Alcatraz *is* an idiot, but he's not enough of an idiot that I felt he didn't know perfectly well that was what would happen if he turned the Lenses off. Sure, there would be some wind resistance (which, yes, is real, but not for the reasons you Hushlanders think), but give

us enough time and we would eventually go the way of
the ice cream cone.

SPLAT.

However, Alcatraz was just enough of an idiot that
I felt he might need to be reminded that falling to our
deaths without a parachute or a glass dragon or anything
of any sort to catch us was a *really bad idea*.

Alcatraz turned and spoke into my ear, sending shiv-
ers down my spine. (Because of what he said, people.
Give me a break; we're miles high in the air. This is not
the spark of our budding romance. Wait, is that a mixed
metaphor?)

"I'm sorry, Bastille," Alcatraz said again.

And then the glasses began to cool against my face,
and we started to fall.

Chapter

6

This seems like a good time to talk about arrogance. And no, I am not like Alcatraz. I will not begin a thought only to make you wait chapters and chapters for me to come back around to explain what I meant. This is my promise to you: on my honor as a knight, I will always finish my

Anyway, arrogance.

Remember back in book three when Alcatraz decided to convince you he was awesome? I hope you believed that, because Alcatraz *is* awesome. But when Alcatraz said that, he didn't mean it. He was exercising a literary technique called *irony*.

Irony is when you say one thing but mean the opposite. Like when I told Alcatraz that his decision to end his autobiography with book five was *brilliant*. And yes, I realize the Free Kingdoms edition is using that as a cover quote.

That's the danger of irony. People who are too stoopid to understand it are free to misquote you at will.

When Alcatraz says he's terrified of kittens, he's deadly serious. But when he said he was awesome, what he wanted you to understand is that he is arrogant. And he is, in this book more than in any other.

I know, I know. He's melted into a puddle of self-pity, which seems like the opposite of arrogance. It might seem like now *I'm* presenting him as a straw man— lacking substance, integrity.

But here's the thing: this time, Alcatraz truly believed he was single-handedly responsible for every evil in the world, and that none of the rest of us were culpable, only him. In short, he thought he was better and smarter and more powerful than the rest of us.

This is arrogance, and also very stoopid. (I seriously feel my IQ drop a few points every time I write that.)

Let me tell you who else might have been able to stop what happened to Attica that day.

Leavenworth, who also failed to realize that Biblioden was hiding among them. Kaz, who hadn't gotten to the altar with them. My mother, who was sworn to protect them. Me, who was in a coma until moments before, but wouldn't have been if I hadn't taken the risk and saved Mokia at the price of not being there to stop Attica's death, which it turns out was far more important to the well-being of all Free Kingdomers, Mokians included.

And, oh yeah, there's one other group that could have stopped all this: *Biblioden and his cult of evil Librarians,* who could have chosen to be, you know, *not* evil.

Here's the thing about arrogance: People like me and Alcatraz like to pretend we're responsible for the bad things other people do. See, we've stopped a lot of bad things from happening. After a while, those kinds of heroics make you feel invincible.

When his father was sacrificed, Alcatraz learned that he wasn't invincible. He discovered that he couldn't stop every bad thing from happening. That's terrifying for a hero to realize—that some horrible things happen no matter what we do.

Like falling inevitably to Earth. (Yes, gravity is physics, and gravity exists. The world would be a very strange place indeed without it, as you will shortly observe.)

I would have screamed as we plummeted toward the ground going about a million miles an hour. But I couldn't scream, because I couldn't breathe. I couldn't do anything except cling to Alcatraz like a demonic kitten as we sped inevitably toward our deaths.

The thing about falling out of the sky is that it's not quick *enough*. You have time to think on the way down about exactly what it's going to feel like to hit the ground and have your body spread out into mush like a spoonful of applesauce. You have time to think about your life choices that led to such a moment. You have time to wonder if your mother was right.

I had time to work on my plan to stop Biblioden, I suppose, but I didn't do that. Yes, without our intervention he was probably going to use the power from Attica to destroy everyone I knew and loved, but that all feels very irrelevant when *your* end is speeding toward you *much* more quickly.

Though I did for a brief second think that if Biblioden would stop being such a shattering *Librarian* and hurry up and explode everyone, I wouldn't have to fall to my death at all.

Stupid Biblioden. No consideration for other people's imminent and terrifying deaths.

I clung to Alcatraz's throat, more for comfort than anything else. No way did I think his body was going to cushion me when we hit the ground. As we fell toward

Earth, the tiny antlike dots of cars on a freeway were getting alarmingly larger. Alcatraz made a sputtering noise against my ear, and I realized I'd tightened my grip around his throat so much that now I really *was* choking him.

I probably should have done him the courtesy of continuing, so that he could pass out before hitting the ground. But I didn't have the presence of mind as the painted lines on the road below became clear.

Alcatraz reached up and tapped his Lenses.

And the frames grew warm against my face again.

The blast of air took an alarming amount of time to overcome the momentum of our fall—long enough that I could see the horrified looks on the faces of the drivers directly below us. Their cars twisted on the road as the wind from the Lenses blew against them. Then, slowly at first, then faster and faster, we rose into the air again. Alcatraz lifted his chin, shooting us back into the air at an angle.

Shattering Glass. Was he planning to bounce us across the continent in great leaps, turning the Lenses on and off to keep them from overheating?

Now more concerned about dying of a heart attack, I loosened my grip on Alcatraz's throat.

"Get us *down!*" I shouted into his ear.

Against my cheek, I felt Alcatraz smile. "Hey!" he shouted. "You wanted me to have an idea!"

I bit my lip so hard I tasted blood. I *had* wanted him to have an idea. And here Alcatraz was, taking charge of our fate, springing us into the air until he couldn't take the (literal) heat anymore and then carefully calculating when to turn the glasses back on so we could fly up on the rebound.

I should have been happy that he was taking action. That was what I'd been trying to achieve, right? And we were headed in the right direction, but even covering miles and miles with each bound as we were, I was still fully aware we were going to have to take a *lot* of leaps to reach the Worldspire.

As my stomach lurched at the bottom of another leap, I screamed at him again. "We can't do this all the way there! Even by airship, that would take— *Aaaaaaaah!*"

That last bit was my scream when we accelerated faster than ever, catapulting into the air so rapidly that the world blurred around us. It was as if the energy Alcatraz was using to power the Lenses was increasing exponentially. For a while, everything around us was a blur.

And then, when Alcatraz finally managed to deactivate the Lenses and we began to decelerate at the top of our arc—

I saw what looked suspiciously like the coastline of the Hushlander continent of Africa.

"Shattering Glass!" I shouted. "What did you do?"

"I think," Alcatraz said in a dazed voice. "I think I may have broken our flight path."

"What?" I said. "You can't have done that. You don't have your Talent."

"I don't know," Alcatraz said. "For a moment, I felt like—"

I clung to him as we plummeted downward again, at a pace that felt downright leisurely compared to how fast we had flown upward before.

What happened next was nonsensical, as things tend to be when the Talents get involved. I didn't know how Alcatraz had done it, but on our next leap the terrain below us changed drastically—we were over an arctic region of some sort, a vast tundra spread out below us. On the next, the kingdom of Mokia appeared—which was on an island in the middle of the Pacific, but on the *other* side of the Worldspire. On the next bounce, the mountains that run like a spine down the center of the Hushlander continent of North America appeared. At least I thought that was what they were.

I hadn't yet managed to catch sight of the Worldspire.

"We can't do this forever!" I shouted at Alcatraz.

"Do you have any better ideas?" he shouted back.

I, as it turned out, did not.

Several bounces along our broken path later, the ocean spread beneath us. I couldn't see more than a few patches of land—

And a tower rising out of the ocean, still miles off. The Worldspire didn't look like much from this distance, just a thin spike of ivory crystal jutting out of the ocean toward the sky, taller than any building or mountain we'd passed.

"It's over there!" I shouted, leaning in the direction of the Worldspire. Alcatraz turned his head to look, and the wind from his glasses propelled us in the opposite direction.

"No!" I shouted, grabbing Alcatraz by the hair and twisting his head back around. "Can you keep our path from breaking again? Because we need to go northwest!" In case he was too stoopid to know which direction that was, I knocked my head against his.

"I'll try!" he said.

On our next gut-wrenching plummet, he did. Instead of following our broken path, we continued to soar over the Pacific. I rested my neck on his shoulder at the top of each bounce, looking for the Worldspire, both to get closer to it and so that we didn't unintentionally

skewer ourselves on the top of it like some kind of Oculator kabob.

There it was. An enormous crystal spike rising out of the ocean and jutting into the atmosphere. As we got closer, I could make out the geometric platform at the bottom, where ships could land when traveling to the spire, and the buildings meant to house the people who did research at the tower. A spiral of wooden scaffolding ran up the sides, leading to a similar (though much smaller in circumference) platform up near the top of the spire, where airships sometimes landed to bring Free Kingdoms scholars to study the tip. I didn't see any airships there now, which perhaps indicated that the Talent had helped us get here ahead of Biblioden.

I didn't know what that meant exactly, but it had to be a good thing for us.

"That way!" I shouted, kicking Alcatraz in the shins like a pony.

"What?" he shouted back.

We hit the bottom of our current arc, and I squeezed my eyes shut and steeled myself for my guts to feel like they were going to fall out of my body. On the upswing— toward the Worldspire, but not as exactly centered as I would have liked—I kicked him again. "*That* way. We need to think about how we're going to stop."

"I'll drop us in the ocean!" Alcatraz shouted. "We can make a smaller arc, and use the Lenses again at the end to slow us down just enough."

That sounded solid, provided the water around the Worldspire wasn't infested with sharks.

Clearly Alcatraz wasn't great at taking horse cues, so I nudged his head with mine again. "Turn *that* way!"

As we fell toward the ocean again, Alcatraz turned to look at the Worldspire, gauging the angle we'd need to take on our next bounce. The waves below scattered in the next blast of air, churning into a deep indentation in the otherwise flat sea as we slowed, then accelerated upward.

I checked the location of the Worldspire. Alcatraz had miscalculated, and at this rate we were headed more toward a chain of islands than toward the spire itself.

We were just beginning our next bounce, so it wasn't too late to correct. "No!" I shouted. "*That* way." I clocked my head against his to emphasize my point.

I may have done so a *bit* too hard. His head turned too sharply, and as we rose in the air again, not yet accelerated to full speed, we started to roll. For a moment we went flying sideways, flipping over in the air until I was hanging down from Alcatraz's back.

And then something flew over the top of Alcatraz's

head, barely missing clipping me in the face before it flew past me and tumbled away through the air.

The Windstormer's Lenses. Our only means of slowing ourselves down as we careened toward the wide ocean below. I had very little time to contemplate the mistakes of my life (the first of which was clearly the decision to let Alcatraz fly us around the world) before we both plunged into the water.

Chapter

Here's the thing about responsibility: no one who is fit to have it really wants it. When you're responsible for other people, you risk letting them down. You risk messing everything up. When your only responsibility every day is to get yourself out of bed and make sure you don't die before you go to sleep again at night, there's nothing to feel guilty about. Still alive? Done and done.

(Though it's somewhat humiliating if you're not. I mean really, what happened? You had *one job*.)

Once you start being responsible for others though, that's when things get complicated.

The ocean water felt oddly warm after thousands

of miles of falling and flight, and I kicked toward the surface, flailing wildly in search of Alcatraz.

Here in the ocean, my Crystin powers *did* help. I reached out to the Mindstone, calling on the swimming abilities of all the knights combined. My muscles didn't change physically, but my movements grew stronger, more sure. Even in my bulky armor, one push against the water sent my body gliding through it ten times as fast as I could have on my own.

I surfaced, gasping for breath, clutching my sword beneath my arm and looking around frantically for Alcatraz.

He bobbed to the surface a moment later, thrashing to keep his head above water. The waves were a lot choppier down here than they had looked from above, and I swam over to him and wrapped his arms around my shoulders. "Hold on!" I shouted, getting a good look around us for the first time.

We were still miles and miles from the Worldspire. Even I couldn't swim all the way to the tower without drowning us both, but we were closer now to the island chain I had seen from the air. I was still shaking from the flight, and more than anything I wanted to put my feet on solid ground. So I made a sensible, non-rash decision my mother would be proud of. I slipped my sword into one of the belt loops on my armor, turned toward the nearest patch of land, and swam, head down in the ocean, pulling Alcatraz behind me. When my knees scraped against rocks, I put my feet down and dragged Alcatraz onto the shore.

You may note I was possibly working against our greater goal of reaching the Worldspire. However, reaching the spire *dead* or *eaten by sharks* would also be counterproductive. Besides, it's Alcatraz's stupid fault. I'm a knight. I'm trained as a protector. He's the one that's supposed to go racing off in stupid directions and nearly get us killed. It's not my fault if I lack the experience to do it correctly.

We climbed up on a beach that seemed somewhat familiar. The color of the sand and the shape of the rock formations led me to believe I had been here sometime before.

Well, that and the enormous wreckage of the once-flying glass dragon that had fallen from the sky when we were first leaving the Hushlands back in book two.

"Well, that's ironic," I said. (You may note that, according to my definition at the beginning of the last chapter, in fact it was not. Al tells me this is because words can have multiple shades of meaning and that's what's wonderful

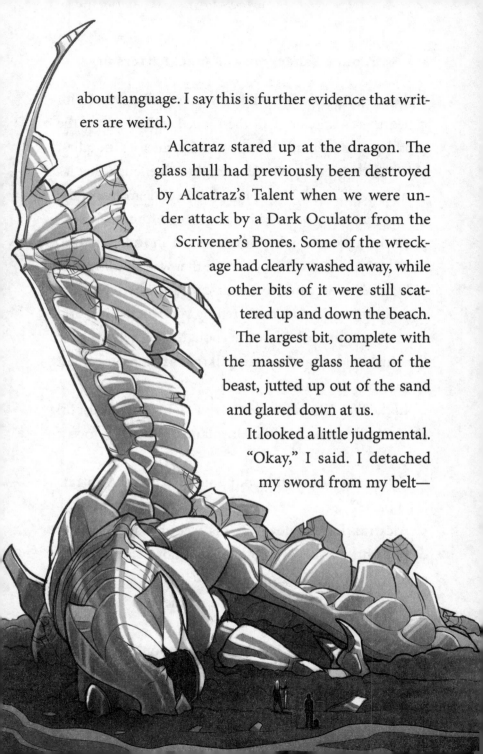

about language. I say this is further evidence that writers are weird.)

Alcatraz stared up at the dragon. The glass hull had previously been destroyed by Alcatraz's Talent when we were under attack by a Dark Oculator from the Scrivener's Bones. Some of the wreckage had clearly washed away, while other bits of it were still scattered up and down the beach.

The largest bit, complete with the massive glass head of the beast, jutted up out of the sand and glared down at us.

It looked a little judgmental.

"Okay," I said. I detached my sword from my belt—

without a proper sheath, I didn't want to walk around with it tied there—and set it in the sand. I looked out at the Worldspire. It was still visible, obviously, since it's the tallest object in the world by a wide margin, tall enough that it's an air travel hazard. That spire, plus the little matter of the several *continents* they need to keep secret from their people, is the reason the Librarians invented air traffic control.

What? You didn't really believe that was for *air traffic,* did you? You all can drive your cars anywhere you like without someone on a radio telling you where to go and when, but you think there are enough planes flying over the Hushlands that they need all that extra protocol not to run into each other?

In the Free Kingdoms, we have a saying: "It's as useful as air traffic control in the Hushlands." Which is to say, not very.

"What happened with your Talent?" I asked Alcatraz. "Is it back?"

Alcatraz looked down at his wet shoes. His pants dripped little rivers onto the sand. "I don't think so," he said. "I don't feel it now."

"But it came back to you for a moment," I said. "And it brought us here."

Alcatraz nodded. "I think so. But I don't know why.

It's hard to describe, but my Talent is like this . . . pressure. It was always there, until suddenly it wasn't."

That made sense, I guess. All that magic building up inside the Smedrys was waiting to go somewhere.

"Could you try to do it again?" I asked. "Maybe you could break the ocean or something. Get us closer to the Worldspire."

Alcatraz closed his eyes, like he was reaching for something inside himself. I imagined it might feel something like when I reached for the power of the Mindstone.

Alcatraz shook his head. "I'm sorry, Bastille," he said. "I don't know why it worked once, but it's not there now."

I sighed. It was frustrating to be so close, but have no way to travel there. Alcatraz still had his briefcase, and I'd managed to hold on to my sword and not cut Alcatraz or myself to pieces with it in the air. Neither of those was going to transport us across the ocean.

"Are the other Lenses okay?" I asked. Not that I saw any particular use for them here, but maybe we could use the Slantviewer's Lenses to see the Worldspire from the perspective of a bird or something.

To get a really good look at Biblioden as he arrived at the spire to vaporize us.

Alcatraz opened the briefcase, checking the Glass-weave pockets. As he touched the pockets, the Glassweave started to glow, and he pulled his fingers back.

I stared at the case. The actual Glassweave was glowing, not the Lenses themselves—though they did seem to be intact.

"Alcatraz," I said. "What in—"

"I don't know," he said. "It happened at the Highbrary too, before my—well, before. I think it has to do with the buildup of energy after I broke the Talents. I think I can use it to power other things, not only Lenses."

I considered that. It would be useful, if we had any glass tech that might still be capable of flying across the water, but all we had was the Glassweave of the briefcase and a very broken airship.

"Well," I said, shaking my head. "Any ideas on what we should do now?" I glanced over my shoulder and found Alcatraz staring blankly out at the ocean.

Then Alcatraz did something else I did not expect.

He fell on his knees and started to cry.

Alcatraz's uselessness was really starting to bother me. It's probably starting to bother you too. No one wants to read about the hero of their story standing there like a lump while the villain rushes off to vaporize the entire free world. Heroes are supposed to be active. They're supposed to throw themselves into the fray, make up crazy plans, and see things through until they *work*. The protagonist of your book, as the real Brandon Sanderson would have told you before he was assassinated by ninjas, is supposed to *protag*.

This, by the way, is a sign of what kind of writer he is. Even *I* know that isn't a word.

I feel I need to remind you at this point that this is not a fantasy novel. It is a completely true account of what happened following the destruction of the Highbrary. One of my purposes in writing this, besides to stop all of you from continually sending hate mail to both Brandon and Alcatraz containing glitter, stink bombs, and sharks (really, if I have to open one more suspicious package containing a shark . . .), is to prove to you that Alcatraz, despite his protesting, is in fact a hero.

This is it, folks. A hero in action. An ordinary person who has just been through something terrible and doesn't know how to go on.

You see, while Alcatraz stood there, his mind kept returning to his father, the altar, and what had happened. (What, you think I'm not allowed to tell you what Alcatraz is thinking? This is a point-of-view violation, you say? Well, allow me to refer you to my aforementioned literary license. I know how Alcatraz was feeling. I've asked him. So there.)

For Alcatraz, the guilt was like a little evil gerbil inside of him, chewing on his intestines. It was a complicated little gerbil. Alcatraz had failed his father—but then, his father had *chosen* to die, rather than let Alcatraz be taken. So was it really a failure?

Also, Alcatraz had spent months resenting Attica, finding the man to be egotistical and generally a poor excuse for a father. But in the end, Attica had sacrificed himself for his son. So now Alcatraz felt bad for all those months of being angry. Except he was still angry, because Attica was such a shattering failure at caring about other people. (His Talent was losing things; it's long been my theory that both he and Shasta, who shared his Talent after they married, lost their humanity years ago, perhaps before Alcatraz was even born. But I suppose we'll never be certain.)

Beyond that, Alcatraz had hardly known his father. So the loss didn't cause Alcatraz as much pain as he thought it should have—and that only made him feel more guilty.

But then there was Grandpa Smedry.

That loss *was* painful. Painful as anything could get. Painful as having your nose smashed by a hammer. Painful as getting a splinter in your eyeball. Painful as someone discovering you secretly love toy ponies. (Shut up. I dress them in armor and give them swords, so it's not what you think.)

Alcatraz kept this turmoil mostly inside. But what you need to realize, and what I didn't know at the time, is that he *was* fighting. He *was* acting. He *was*—if you must make up your own words—protagging. It was his own little war going on inside, but the fate of the world itself depended upon that war. If you start to think he's being sullen or whiny . . . well, you're probably right. But do try to remember that he'd watched his father die mere hours before. All in all, he was doing pretty well.

NOW WE'RE GOING TO STOP TALKING ABOUT ALCATRAZ IN THE ABSTRACT AND GO BACK TO US STANDING ON THE ISLAND. THERE WAS NOT A WAR BEING FOUGHT ON THE ISLAND. I WISH THERE HAD BEEN; THEN I WOULD HAVE HAD SOMETHING TO FIGHT.

You see that?

You see what I did just above? That's called a *transition*. It's where an author is describing one scene, and then manages to *skillfully* and *imperceptibly* bring us back into another scene after yammering on for a while. (*Yammering*, I assure you, is not a made-up word.) That was *smooth*, wasn't it? You barely noticed.

Man, I'm getting good at this writing thing.

It might surprise you to know that I'm not much of a crier. (Shut up. I said it *might*. Like if you're one of those people who picks up book six in a series and starts reading a third of the way through. And if that's you, might I ask again: What's wrong with you?)

Alcatraz, for that matter, isn't either. Yes, I knew that the tears were about his dad and his guilt and the fact that we could now see the Worldspire but not reach it. Our odds of stopping Biblioden from here were pretty minimal.

At that moment, I myself felt defeated. I felt like I wanted to fall to my own knees (which were startlingly shaky postflight) and sob right along with him.

"It's okay," I said, though I knew perfectly well that it wasn't okay. "Or, the only way for it to *be* okay is for us to figure this out. Okay?"

And that's what I talked like before I was forced to write the word *stoopid* a half dozen times. What do you suppose I would sound like now?

"No," Alcatraz said. "I'm sorry. I can't help you."

You are no doubt starting to feel that it's the point in the story where Alcatraz should snap out of his funk and return to his plucky self and save the day. After all, I said this was a narrative that was going to prove to you that Alcatraz is, despite what he thinks, a hero.

But I'll remind you that this is not a work of fiction that can constrain itself to plot structures and other artistic devices. This is a piece of journalism, a true account of the events as they happened. So yes, we really did go flying across the world propelled by only a pair of overclocked Windstormer's Lenses. And no, this exhilarating experience did nothing to improve Alcatraz's mood.

Or mine.

The trouble was, at this point Alcatraz was feeling not just guilt, but shame. Shame is to guilt what a Gak is to a dragon. Shame is when you stop feeling bad about things you've done or failed to do, and start feeling bad about who you *are.*

"We can see the shattering Worldspire," I said. "There has to be a way for us to get from here to there."

"I'm a failure, Bastille," Alcatraz said. "I've failed everyone. My grandfather. My dad. My mother. *You.* Everyone."

"We still have three pairs of Lenses," I said.

"We left your mother and Kaz and the others to be shot at by Librarians."

"I'm pretty sure they escaped," I said. "They were in a much better position to do so than we were, and Kaz may have lost his Talent, but my mother is still a Knight of Crystallia. She'll have gotten him out."

"—and now everyone in the Free Kingdoms is going

to explode, or incinerate, or cease to exist, and it's all because I didn't fight Biblioden. I didn't stop him. I let him take my father, and if Attica were here he'd know how to stop it, and if I'd died instead of him I could have saved you all."

Okay. Now he was starting to get to me. Yes, I understood the reasons he was feeling the way he did, but obnoxious is obnoxious, motivated or not.

Clearly I wasn't the person he needed to get him back on track, to help him see his way out of this dark pit he'd fallen into. If Leavenworth were here, he would have known how to do it. For a moment I thought about shouting, "Hustling Husbergs, boy!" and following it with something equally nonsensical and preposterous.

But I'm not Leavenworth, and I now stood in the middle of the mess I'd made by trying to act like a Smedry. This time, I was going to play to my strengths. I stayed on task.

"Maybe if you tell me how you broke the Talents," I said, "maybe we could figure out how to get your Talent working normally again."

"I can't," Alcatraz said, prostrating himself across the sand. "I hated my Talent my whole life, and now it hates me."

That, I thought, was a bit dramatic. "Your Talent isn't

a person," I said. "Though *I* am going to start hating you if you don't snap out of this and save the rest of your wallowing in misery for *after* we figure out *how not to get murdered by Biblioden.*"

Alcatraz sat up and glowered at me. (Alcatraz says that even if *glowered* is my new favorite word, it's a "money word," and therefore I should limit its usage. I say, if I'm being paid for using fancy words, I might undergo to utilize them at supplementary intervals, *n'est-ce pas?*)

"It's hopeless," he said in an irritated tone. "We're all going to die."

"Yeah," I said. "We definitely are if you keep sitting there whining instead of trying to *help me.*"

"Aren't you *listening?* Why are you still acting like I'm going to stop this from happening? I'm not. I can't stop anything, Bastille. I can't. I'm nothing."

If I hadn't just taken a terrifying flight across many parts of the world and then landed on a beach that *we had crashed on before,* I might have been able to see that Alcatraz crying and venting his feelings was progress of sorts, and much healthier than sitting around bottling it all up and staring into space. But in that moment, I didn't care what had happened to put him in such a sorry state.

"Get up," I said.

Alcatraz, to his credit, got up. His head hung and

his shoulders hunched and his eyes stared at his once-shiny shoes, but he did get up. Slowly.

I walked over, got right in his face, and lifted him by the front of his very wet shirt. Again. Only this time I kept lifting until he was hanging in front of me, his shoes dripping down onto the sand. "Shut up!" I said. "*No one* talks about my *friend* like that."

I must have sounded like I meant it, because Alcatraz did shut up. He stared down at me in shock, his hair hanging over his forehead and dripping inconveniently into my eye.

And then his face crumpled, and he started to cry again.

That's when I lost patience. I yanked his face close to mine and growled at him.

A lady needs to practice a good growl. They can be useful in so many situations. Forget those magazines with their "helpful" advice on picking promenade dresses. Trust Bastille. Learn to growl. Way more useful.

Alcatraz blinked. "That's . . . a rather good growl."

"Thanks," I said. "It's number thirty-seven. I'm quite proud of it."

"You have *thirty-seven* different growls?"

"Fifty-two," I said. "A girl needs to be multigrowlual these days. So, are you done being stoopid?"

"Because you growled at me?"

"Clearly."

Now, before you get any ideas, I should mention that that last section—no matter how it might have looked—did *not* involve subtle romantic tension. I'm totally incapable of subtlety. Haven't you noticed?

"Do you remember when I was depressed in the Royal Archive (not a library)?" I said. "And you found me rolled up in a ball on the floor?"

"Yeah," he said, his eyes growing wide. His face was very close to mine. My face was getting hot, probably because of the sun shining down on us. I'm sure that was it.

Somehow, Alcatraz managed not to look me in the

eye. But he couldn't get away, not unless he wanted to take off his shirt. Once, he would have simply broken it.

How the mighty had fallen.

"So?" I asked. "Talk to me."

"About what?"

"I dunno," I said. "Feelings and stuff."

I was definitely getting better at this empathy thing.

"I let my father die, Bastille," Alcatraz said softly. "No, it's *worse* than that. I told Biblioden to take him instead of me. I'm a coward."

"Alcatraz," I said, "I've seen you stand up to ghosts, giant robots, and *kittens*. You're not a coward."

"Then why did I let them take him instead?"

"Probably because you wanted to live," I said. "Like any normal human being. We like to think we'll always jump up and be self-sacrificing, but it's hard to be in control of yourself in a moment like that."

Alcatraz nodded, but didn't say anything. I thought about threatening him again but decided against it. "Tell me what happened," I said softly.

He talked slowly, in a hush, but he forced it out. The story of coming to the Highbrary—of which I'd only heard bits and pieces from my mother during our escape—and finding out that Biblioden had been hiding

among them all along. And then the capture, Leavenworth Smedry being shot, and . . . the altar.

It was a tough story to hear, and I could see how it was
crushing him to speak the words. "And then he made
me choose," Alcatraz finally finished, his eyes unfo-
cused. "Choose my own life or that of my father. And . . .
Bastille . . . my father spoke at the same time as I did. I
said, 'Take him,' and he said, 'Take me.' He chose to sacrifice himself, while I panicked. In the end, *he* was the
hero. And I failed him."

"It doesn't matter what you said," I told him. "I can
guarantee Biblioden was going to take your father, no
matter what. He saw Attica as the more dangerous threat.
You couldn't have done anything to protect your father."

"That doesn't change the fact that I am a terrible
person," he whispered. "In that moment, I revealed what
I really am, Bastille."

"So what?"

"So, it means I'm worthless," Alcatraz said. "That I'm
not a hero, like everyone wants to pretend."

I shook my head at him. "No, Alcatraz. It means you're
human. I'm not going to tell you that you did the right
thing—because I don't think there *was* a right thing to
do at a time like that. Nobody should ever have to make
a decision like Biblioden forced upon you. You're not a

coward or some villain because you reacted the same way everyone else would have."

My words didn't seem to comfort him much, which made me angry. Both at him and at myself. I want to come up with some great description here, but the truth is, he just looked *sad*.

"I'm sorry, Bastille," he said. "I'm not a hero."

I'd had enough. I dropped him in the sand and stalked away. I knew I should be nicer. I knew I should talk him through it. But at this point, I was just so *furious* that he couldn't even *try* to think our way over to the World-spire. We'd already figured out how to travel around the shattering *world*. A few more miles shouldn't be so much to ask.

I stomped up the beach toward the tree line. The border between trees and sand grew thick with tall grass behind the ruins of the *Dragonaut*. If I couldn't talk sense into Alcatraz, I was at least going to find someplace private to relieve myself.

Wait, am I not supposed to talk about that? Alcatraz says I'm not allowed to mention bodily functions in books. Shattering Glass, Al, it's not like I was going to give them the details.

So, as I was reaching down to unbuckle my belt, and—oh, *fine*—as I was standing out in the middle of a grove of trees for no discernible reason whatsoever like people totally do when they've just flown across the world by leaps and bounds but have *no* biological needs whatsoever, the grass started rustling.

I don't mean a small patch of grass. I don't mean a few fronds here or there. I mean the entire line of grass that edged the jungle and continued deep into the trees started to rustle at once. Some of it shifted this way and some of it shifted that way, as if an enormous creature were slithering beneath the grass, coiled around and around itself beneath the foliage.

My stomach dropped, and I nearly peed my pants. (Okay, so if I'm going to urinate *in my body armor*, it's allowed in the book, but if I was going to do it in a bush like a normal person who finds themselves stranded in the middle of nowhere, I'm not supposed to mention it? You writer people are *weird*.)

And then, across the field—out of a thin patch of grass—emerged a large yellow spike attached to a blue scaly hide.

"Gak!" I shouted, and ran back to Alcatraz as quickly as I could go.

Alcatraz was back to lying in the sand in his tuxedo, looking like a corpse who washed up onshore. (What, was I supposed to make a joke there? Fine. He looked like the corpse of *a comedian* washed up on the shore. Happy?)

"Gak!" I said again as I approached.

"I heard you," Alcatraz said. "And whatever you're Gakking about, trust me, it's not as bad as the rest of what I've seen today."

I crouched down beside him, keeping my eyes on the tall grass. "No, you idiot," I said as the grass began to part. "Gak!"

A long, serpentine head, kind of like if a python had an alligator's babies, only *really, really big,* slipped out of the grass. The spines of its bulbous body arched out of the grass at intervals behind it (though they were neither particularly utilized nor supplementary).

"Gak," I said, more softly this time.

Alcatraz sat up, looking concerned for a brief moment before fading back into existential ennui. (I'm liking these money words. This book is going to be worth a *fortune.*)

And then the Gak turned its scaly head in our direction and grinned, showing off its many rows of teeth.

Chapter

9

By this point, you're probably thinking of guilt as a bad thing. This is not true. Imagine that your mother has just bought a candy bar. (My editor suggested that perhaps your mother did something more sweet and personal, like baking a pumpkin pie. The thought of my mother baking a pie is beyond the scope of my imagination, so I asked Alcatraz what he thought.

We decided to go with the candy bar.)

Your mother bought this candy bar, but it isn't for you. (Ah yes. There's a mother both Alcatraz and I can relate to.) In fact, it is for your older brother. (I lose Alcatraz here, because he also lacks the imagination to pretend he has an older brother. I, unfortunately, don't have to imagine.)

Now pretend that you've eaten this candy bar intended for your brother. At this point, one of a few things will happen. You might feel bad about it, and decide not to do things like that in the future. You might feel bad about it, and keep right on eating other people's candy bars because you have no self-control. Or, you might *not* feel bad about it, and decide that eating other people's candy bars is totally okay with you.

Now imagine the candy bar *is* your mother.

See what happens when you don't feel guilty?

Matricide and cannibalism.

I really think I'm getting the hang of this metaphor thing.

"We need straw," I said.

"That creature looks like it was drawn by Dr. Seuss," Alcatraz whispered.

"Doctor who?" I asked.

"No, that's someone different. But now that I think about it, he clearly had his hands on some Expander's Glass."

"*Alcatraz*," I snapped. "Focus. That is a Gak, and we don't have any straw."

Alcatraz rolled his eyes. At a Gak. From the looks of the way it was snuffling around at the edge of the rocks, a *hungry* Gak.

You Free Kingdomers, I'm sure, are astonished right now. But you have to remember that Alcatraz had never seen a Gak. He'd never even fully heard of one. So while you are imagining images from *A Nation Without Straw* or *Garrison and the Great White Gak*, he was seeing a creature that looked like it might have been drawn by a beloved children's book illustrator.

(To be fair, Alcatraz has since acquainted me with Dr. Seuss, and his drawings do bear a striking similarity to the anatomy of the Gak. Though I still don't understand what he has to do with Expander's Glass.)

"How would straw help?" Alcatraz asked.

"Gaks are terrified of straw," I said.

This was an oversimplification, of course. You Free Kingdomers know that Gaks used to love straw. Back in the seventeenth century, they would return to their lairs after a day of pillaging and eating all the people they could get their claws on, and then down a bushel or two of straw to aid in their digestion.

But then something happened that forever altered the intestinal tract of Gak-kind.

Soap.

See, Free Kingdomers and Hushlanders alike have been bathing since ancient times. But the popularity of soap worldwide is something of a recent phenomenon. The fact is that soap does terrible things to the digestive systems of Gaks. They started needing more and more straw to settle their stomachs. They started eating whole fields of grain just to get at the stalky part of the plant.

As a result, people started starving, and Gaks had fewer people to eat, and in general everyone was miserable. There was a lot of talk about going to war, but the Gaks didn't want to fight their food source, and no one with any kind of sense in their head wants to go to war with a Gak.

Until renowned explorer Polunsky Ansel brokered the Great Gak Treaty, in which the Gaks promised never to touch a single piece of straw again. In exchange, the human population promised to stop playing accordions, the sound of which makes Gaks crazy. (Along with everyone else.)

If, by chance, you catch a Gak in the act of touching straw, the treaty stipulates that the Gak is required to do you a service, and anyone with half a brain asks the Gak for the service of not being eaten.

Gaks *hate* doing this service. But the arrangement serves a triple purpose. Fewer people eaten by Gaks. Fewer Gaks with indigestion. And more straw for the rest of us to keep around to ward off Gaks.

I mean, what else would you use straw for?

"That Gak," Alcatraz whispered, "is in a *field* of straw. It doesn't look very frightened to me."

"That's *not* straw," I said. "That is grass. There's an agricultural difference."

Alcatraz raised an eyebrow at me, as if he was waiting for me to tell him what it was.

"This is not the time," I said to him. Which was definitely because we were being stared down by a Gak and not because I didn't have any idea how the finer points of the Great Gak Treaty split hairs on the issue of straw versus grass.

"Well," the Gak said. "Are you finished?"

"Gak!" Alcatraz said. "It talks."

"Of course it talks," I said. "How do you think Polunsky brokered a treaty with them if they don't talk?"

Alcatraz looked at me like I'd lost my mind, and I remembered that while I'd told you the long version of the story, I hadn't told him.

This was still not the time. "Finished with what?" I asked it.

The Gak slithered closer, the first large bulb of its caterpillar-like body protruding from the grass. Gaks swallow people whole and digest them in the sacs along their body over weeks, sometimes months. They can digest as many people at a time as they have sacs to carry them.

And no, no one has ever cut their way out of a Gak from the inside. Gaks are not stupid. They always kill you first. I'd tell you how, but my editor already thinks I'm too violent.

"Talking," the Gak said. "I wasn't going to interrupt your conversation to eat you. I do have manners."

"Bastille," Alcatraz said, "aren't you going to fight it?"

I looked at my sword, lying in the sand. It survived the flight and the long swim here, but if I used it to fight a Gak, I wasn't going to last thirty seconds. "No," I said. "I read in *To Hunt the Gak* that twelve Crystins once fought a Gak, all together, with a terrain advantage. And they all died."

"It's probably just a story," Alcatraz said. "It doesn't look that scary. Like a smaller dragon."

Spoken by someone who has never had to best a dragon in one-on-one combat. "It is *not* just a story," I told him. "It's a work of nonfiction. And *our* nonfiction sections are true, unlike in the Hushlands, where your books are divided into lies the Librarians want you to believe and lies that they don't care about either way."

The Gak stared at us again, like it was waiting for us to finish.

"So, what are we going to do?" Alcatraz asked. "Stand here and let it eat us?"

"I'm tempted to let it eat *you*," I said. "For all the help you've been."

"I got us out of the Hushlands," Alcatraz said. "That's something."

It was something. As was him snapping back at me when I provoked him. It was a very good sign that would have encouraged me much more if I wasn't staring at a Gak that had already declared its intention to eat me.

"A straw," I said out of the side of my mouth. "We need a piece of straw."

"There isn't any straw on this island," the Gak said. "Don't you think I checked before I decided to settle here?"

It probably did.

"What about a strawberry?" Alcatraz asked.

"Won't work," the Gak said.

"Why?" I asked Alcatraz. "Do you have one?"

Alcatraz shrugged. "I'm just trying to understand the rules."

"The rules are, if I touch a straw, I owe you the service of not eating you. Or another service if you prefer, though it's never happened to my knowledge."

I would imagine not.

"Are you sure that grass isn't straw?" I asked.

Alcatraz gave me a self-satisfied look. That was an even better sign. If I wasn't sure we were about to be eaten by a Gak, I might have been happy about it.

"All right, idiot," I said. "Think of something."

Alcatraz appeared to actually think. And then he looked hopefully up at the Gak.

"Please don't eat us," he said. "That would be strawful."

Oh no. "Alcatraz," I said, "I don't think—"

"You do look rather *distrawt*," the Gak offered.

"And this conversation is getting strawkward," Alcatraz added. "It would be strawsome if you would let us go."

They both looked at me expectantly.

"I'm not helping," I said. "I would rather be eaten by a Gak than pun my way out of this." It might not be as ill-advised as trying to best a Gak at riddles, but a girl has to draw the line somewhere if she's going to maintain her self-respect.

"It's quite the strawggle, keeping up with you," the Gak said to Alcatraz.

"And you," Alcatraz said, "are a strawng opponent."

Shattering Glass. *Fine.* I'll admit it. I gave in. "This," I said, "is the final straw."

Alcatraz nodded somberly. "You did get the short straw, ending up with me."

The Gak made a choking noise, and I edged toward my sword.

And then I realized the Gak was laughing.

"All right," it said when it stopped. "Since you two have been so entertaining, I'll let you choose who's going to be eaten first."

Alcatraz immediately volunteered.

I feel it's important to mention here that my efforts to get Alcatraz to do something in Chapter Eight were *not* because of some kind of mystical "he's the Chosen One"–type nonsense. That's the sort of thing you'd find in a silly fantasy novel, and not in a completely true account of actual events like this.

I had faith in Alcatraz because he'd proven to me that he deserved that faith. Yes, he was a drooling nitwit at the moment, but being a nitwit had never held him back in the past. The drooling part was a bonus feature, like discovering that your sword came with an extra sheath to better match different outfits. We could use him to water potted plants now, for example.

Anyway, I trusted him. He was the one who had heard

the Scrivener's plans, had read Attica's notes—even just a little bit. If anyone could figure a way out of this mess, it would be him. And I came to that conclusion on my own.

There's no such thing as a Chosen One. Only people who are put in difficult situations and do their best.

I stared down at Alcatraz. I can't say I was surprised, and I also can't say I was angry. Not because I wasn't, but because I'm angry so often that I'm running out of new ways to describe it. Hang on, let me check my thesaurus.

I felt *apoplectic* with *wrath*. Cha-ching!

"Idiot," I said. "That's not helping."

"I'm sorry, Bastille," Alcatraz said. "But if this is my chance to redeem myself for—"

"Being eaten first is not redemption!" I yelled at him. "Being eaten first is stupid!"

"It's actually pretty cowardly," said the Gak. "Because the person who gets eaten second has to watch."

Alcatraz's face fell, like he truly thought he needed to volunteer to watch me be eaten in order to not be a total failure at life.

Shattering Glass. We did not have time for this.

"Fine," I said. "Enjoy him. I hope he tastes delicious." I turned, picked up my sword and the briefcase of Lenses, and marched down the beach, hissing at Alcatraz to *stall*. I heard the grass rustling as the Gak advanced on him.

At the very least, this particular Gak seemed to enjoy toying with its prey before doing that thing my editor says is far too dark for this book. But in the interest of journalism, I feel I must tell you that Gaks have a habit of ███████████████████████████████████████
███████████████████████████████████████

Well, there. Now you know.

Alcatraz did, at least, seem motivated to stall. "Are you interested in astrawnomy?" he asked the Gak. "I don't want to strawng-arm you into anything, but I feel that if we don't adequately get to know each other, it might lead to catastrawphy."

I stomped toward the *Dragonaut*, scanning the craft for anything that might have been left behind. A drinking straw, perhaps. A hat made out of straw. Australia had been on board, and she has very strange taste in clothes.

If anything like that had been left behind, the Gak had long since removed it.

"If you eat us, the world is going to end," Alcatraz said. "Did we mention that?"

The rustling stopped. I kicked over a glass tooth

that had once been mounted on the prow of the ship, and then turned around.

The Gak was a mere ten feet from Alcatraz now, and Alcatraz had scrambled to his feet and backed up so his heels were in the surf. The Gak had drawn itself up like a cobra, and stared down at him as if prepared to strike.

"Is that so?" the Gak asked. It didn't sound particularly convinced.

"It is," I said. "Biblioden, head of the evil Librarians, is headed toward the Worldspire right now, and he's going to use the power of the Incarna to kill everyone."

The Gak gave a dubious snort, but it did turn and look out at the Worldspire.

I motioned for Alcatraz to come closer to me and the glass ship. He looked ready to leap into the ocean to get away, but I already knew that wouldn't work. Gaks can swim. If they couldn't, how would this one have gotten to the island to begin with?

Alcatraz moved slowly up the beach toward me. "Is that him now?"

A large blimp-shaped glass craft hung in the sky near the Worldspire. It had to be Librarian-made. Any Free Kingdomer would have come up with a more imaginative design.

"Yes," I said. "Yes, it probably is."

Alcatraz's shoulders slumped. "That's it, then," he said. "We're too late."

As you may have noticed, this was not true, as Alcatraz and I were not yet vapor. And Alcatraz at least had the sense to step up near me, where I might stand a shattering chance of keeping him alive once the distraction stopped.

The Gak turned back to Alcatraz, and scowled at us when it realized we'd moved farther away. We were only a few feet from the main hull of the *Dragonaut* now, though it wasn't as if we could hide behind it and hope the Gak would go away.

"Why would he want to destroy the world?" the Gak asked.

"Technically only the Free Kingdomers will die," Alcatraz said. "But that's your food source, isn't it? After that, you'll have no one to eat."

The Gak shrugged. "Hushlanders taste fine," it said. "I have a cousin in a lake up in Scotland who does quite well for herself."

Then three things happened at once. First, the Gak raised itself up into striking position again, the bulbs of its body pulsing ominously. Second, I whipped my sword up across my body in a defensive stance. Third, Alcatraz stumbled backward, tripping over a large glass shard and tearing his sopping-wet tuxedo pants. He reached out to keep from falling over, and grabbed the base of the *Dragonaut's* tail.

The glass began to glow where he touched it.

I stepped between Alcatraz and the Gak. I didn't think I could defeat it, but if it was a choice between fighting it and simply letting it kill Alcatraz—last living heir to the Smedry line, and also my *friend*—I was going to at least make it difficult.

"Alcatraz," I said, "what are you doing?"

"I have an idea."

This should have been terrible news, after his last idea, but I had to admit I found flying across the world preferable to being eaten by a Gak.

The Gak reached the apex of its strike pose, and I readied my sword. And then I jumped to the side when the pieces of glass dragon beneath my feet started twisting and unearthing themselves from the sand.

"Gak!" I shouted as a chunk of the *Dragonaut's* belly emerged.

The Gak struck at Alcatraz, but he ducked around the back of the glass dragon (a strategy I had clearly underestimated). "Get in!" he shouted.

"What?" I yelled back.

Alcatraz didn't respond, but through the glass hull I could see he had climbed inside the *Dragonaut* and was moving toward the engine room.

The Gak reared up again, and I ducked in through a hole in the *Dragonaut*'s hull just as a wave of energy hummed around me, buzzing through every bit of the glass. I wished I had Grappler's Glass boots, because I had a feeling Alcatraz was about to do something crazy.

Again.

The Gak snaked around the outside of the hull, as if it were about to squeeze the *Dragonaut* to bits.

"Alcatraz!" I shouted. "The wings have been destroyed. We don't even have an engine. It broke in the crash."

It didn't matter. The glowing energy spread out across the stumps of the *Dragonaut*'s wings, reconstructing them out of pure energy. The Gak screamed as the ship took flight, and I scrambled away from the hole in the hull, not sure if the energy would hold me in if I touched it.

As we lifted into the air, the Gak's exposed belly slithered across the hole.

And I lunged forward with my sword, slashing it from one side to the other.

I didn't score it deep enough to be a killing blow, but Shattering Glass, that felt good. As did the high-pitched

squealing sound the Gak made as it recoiled, lost its hold on the *Dragonaut,* and went tumbling down into the water below.

I blinked. We were over the water. I was once again flying in an unstable craft—though I had to admit this beat clinging to Alcatraz's back while we free-fell out of the air. I climbed the rest of the way to the engine room to find Alcatraz kneeling on the floor where the engine used to be, both palms pressed against it. Streams of energy poured out of him and into the glass, and the ship bobbed as the wings lifted us higher and higher into the air.

"What did you do?" I asked. "It doesn't have a silimatic engine anymore."

"I think," Alcatraz said, coming as close to smiling as I'd seen since waking up in the Highbrary, "that I *am* the silimatic engine."

That should be impossible. But Alcatraz had been doing impossible things with glass for all the time I'd known him. He'd had some theory about silimatic technology working the same way as Oculator magic.

I'd doubted that he could be right, but if it got us to the Worldspire (and away from the murderous Gak), I'd take it.

I pressed against the solid glass part of the hull, looking out at the Worldspire, which was growing slowly larger on the horizon. "Biblioden beat us there," I said. "We don't know what's waiting for us."

"I know," Alcatraz said. "But we're about to find out."

Chapter

• 11 •

Alcatraz has informed me that I don't get paid more for "money words." He says this is just an expression for words that are unnecessarily long and complicated. In fact, if I were being paid *by* the word, short words would be more lucrative, because I could write more of them in less time. A Librarian scheme if I've ever heard one.

In that case, I will try to use short words. Very short. Tiny. OK?

We flew. Spire got big. Ship glowed. Think they saw us? Yep. They did.

No good. Shot down. Glass broke. Crash. Ouch.

(Alcatraz now informs me that I'm not being paid by the word. Rather, I'm being paid *per copy*. So I have a favor to ask you. Please kindly eat your book and buy another. Thank you in advance.)

So there we were, sitting in the remains of the *Dragonaut,* now shattered into bits a second time by our crash into the Worldspire. I scrambled out of the broken glass, hauling Alcatraz with me by the back of his very tattered jacket.

We'd landed on the platform near the top of the tower, with the last stretch of the Worldspire jutting sharply up in the center. Above us, around the top of the spire, was a small crow's nest with a winding staircase leading up to it.

The platform around the spire stretched about thirty feet in all directions—large enough for our ship to have crash-landed without sliding off the side of the spire and landing miles below in the ocean.

And also plenty of room for the Librarian blimp to have landed much less dramatically. A half dozen Librarians waited for us, several wearing Warrior's Lenses. They were led by a Librarian wearing a pair of Lenses with a sickly green tint.

I didn't see Biblioden anywhere, but they did have an Oculator.

"Orders, Etna?" one of the Librarians called.

"Get the Crystin," the Oculator said. Then she smiled. "I'll take the Smedry."

We'll see about that. I tossed the case with the Lenses at Alcatraz, and stepped between him and the Librarians, holding my sword with both hands. That wasn't necessary—I had the grace and strength of the whole Crystin order behind me, so I didn't need two arms to swing a sword. But I look menacing that way, and a girl can never appear *too* menacing.

Alcatraz fumbled with the case, and I saw him retrieve the Slantviewer's Lenses, the Tracker's Lenses, and, most importantly, the Oculator's Lenses—good for sensing Oculatory auras, and also for general defense.

He put the Oculator's Lenses on, and I grinned.

Alcatraz was back. He turned toward the Oculator.

The other Librarians charged me, and I waited until they were almost upon me to swing my sword and step to the side. I hit one of the Librarians with the flat of my blade, applying enough pressure to fling her away, and reached out with one hand, plucking the Warrior's Lenses from the face of the other.

I smiled and put them on. I hadn't had a good pair of Warrior's Lenses since I woke up back in the Highbrary. They're one of the few pairs of Lenses that can be used by non-Oculators, and while my Crystin shard offers me more in the way of defensive powers, I never mind the extra boost.

The Librarians recovered quickly, but I dispatched them both without much effort. The other four backed up toward the center of the spire, realizing, I'm sure, that their Warrior's Lenses weren't going to cut it against a full Crystin.

The air around me buzzed, and I looked up at the crow's nest at the top of the spire, concerned that Biblioden might be up there, but the space was empty.

"I've always wanted to duel a Smedry," the Librarian Oculator said.

Oh no. Alcatraz stood a real chance in a battle against a Dark Oculator right now, his powers being as strong as they were. And there was still his Talent, which was eluding us, but which had come to his aid when we needed it most.

But an Oculator's Duel? It was a kind of formal fight, where two Oculators stood across from each other, taking turns stacking Lenses and channeling power through them, until one of the Oculators could no longer hold off the opposing power and had to yield. Alcatraz only had three Lenses, and none of them were particularly offensive—though I knew Leavenworth always said that utility Lenses could be better in a duel than the more direct offensive choices, if you knew how to use them.

Alcatraz didn't. As far as I knew, he'd never been in an Oculator's Duel, and had seen only one take place— between Leavenworth and Blackburn the Dark Oculator during our first library infiltration back in book one.

I turned around to find Alcatraz standing with his feet planted, looking determinedly at the Dark Oculator through his Oculator's Lenses.

"Alcatraz," I said, "you—"

Shattering Glass. I couldn't announce to the Dark Oculator that Alcatraz had never done this before, though that was going to become obvious quickly. I still hadn't seen Biblioden, and I was beginning to think he wasn't here yet. What we'd run into was a kind of vanguard, coming to prepare the way.

Which meant we needed to deal with this Oculator— Etna, they said her name was—and fast.

The four remaining Librarians took advantage of my distraction and chose that moment to all charge me at once. I spun and fended them off with a downward swing, then advanced, separating two from the group and backing them up toward the edge of the tower. I cut them down and then wheeled around to face the other two.

An aura of power radiated from Etna, who had raised a pair of gray Lenses to her eyes—I thought those were Concussor's Lenses—stacking them over her first pale green set.

Alcatraz stood perfectly still as a beam of white-hot

power shimmered out from Etna and slammed into him. Etna lowered her hand, and the second set of Lenses hovered in the air in front of her, held in place by the concentrated power that flowed between them.

It was too late for me to interfere. If I did, the excess energy that was currently blocked by Alcatraz's Oculator's Lenses could vaporize me.

There are a lot of ways this story could end, and a staggering number of them involve me being vaporized. This should be starting to alarm you.

Alcatraz had his Slantviewer's Lenses hooked to the front of his shirt, and he began to raise his Tracker's Lenses to his eyes.

"Not those!" I yelled. Those were some of the easiest Lenses to use, and therefore the least powerful in the traditional sense. They would be no use in a duel.

I kept my sword out between me and the remaining Librarians, backing up until I was close enough to Alcatraz that the beam of Oculatory power reflecting off his Lenses made my bones rattle.

Technically it was Alcatraz's turn to add a Lens of his own, but when he declined to add the Tracker's Lenses, it gave leave for Etna to add a third pair. She smiled and pulled out a set of frosty-blue Frostbringer's Lenses. An icy beam of light shot through the three pairs hovering in front of Etna's face. Alcatraz took a staggered step backward, but held strong.

No normal Oculator could hold off so many powerful offensive Lenses with only a pair of Oculator's Lenses, but Alcatraz wasn't a normal Oculator. If he ever had been, he'd done too many impossible things to be considered one now. He might be able to do more with one pair of Lenses than the Dark Oculator could do with a dozen.

A drop of sweat ran down the bridge of Alcatraz's nose. The Dark Oculator took a step forward, and Alcatraz took another step back. His glasses were beginning to glow slightly, and not from the defensive aura. They were overheating, like the Windstormer's Lenses had before Alcatraz was forced to remove them.

Alcatraz didn't have long. Those Lenses were going to melt on his face, burning him or becoming useless. He couldn't take them off without getting blown backward by an enormous blast of power, and even if he managed to keep them on, the Dark Oculator seemed intent on pushing Alcatraz off the Worldspire, where he'd fall for miles until he slammed into the ocean.

I had failed too many Smedrys. I wasn't going to let that happen to Alcatraz. Not on my watch. "Alcatraz," I said, "see if you can focus some of that excess power. If you can push it through the Lenses, you can use it to block the attack and use the power up in the process."

Alcatraz's brow furrowed behind his Lenses, and his eyes nearly went crossed as he focused. More sweat fell from his forehead, but the icy beam pushed back several inches.

"It's your turn, Smedry!" Etna called. "Unless you want to yield."

Shattering Glass. How many pairs of offensive Lenses was she going to produce?

And Alcatraz only had one more. The Slantviewer's Lenses.

Oh. "Listen carefully," I said to Alcatraz. "You're going to win this."

Alcatraz's expression faltered for a second, as if he didn't believe me. But he kept focusing his power through the Lenses at Etna, which was all I needed him to do for the moment.

"Use the Slantviewer's Lenses," I said quietly. I was willing to bet that Etna hadn't figured out what those were, and so she wouldn't be expecting this.

Alcatraz nodded and raised the Lenses, putting them in front of the Oculator's Lenses and letting go hesitantly, as if expecting them to fall. Caught in the beam of power, the Lenses hovered in front of his face. Alcatraz grunted, and more power pushed through, shoving the Dark Oculator back.

"You've got this," I said.

The power of the Dark Oculator inched closer. If the Dark Oculator was confused about what Alcatraz was doing, she didn't show it. She reached into her pocket and withdrew a set of Lenses with an autumn-orange tint.

"Wait," Alcatraz said. "I'm not—"

"No, let her," I said. The Slantviewer's Lenses worked by transferring the gaze of the person you marked as a target, and making it your own. At the moment, Etna's gaze was full of Oculatory power. All Alcatraz had to do was harness it, and the more power the Dark Oculator pushed at Alcatraz, the more he would have to aim right back at her.

"Mark her as your target, Alcatraz," I said.

He gave the barest of nods, and reached up to tap the Slantviewer's Lenses.

"Okay," I said. "You'll have to look down at yourself to mark yourself. As soon as you look away, her power will start to get through, so make it quick."

Alcatraz drew a deep breath, and Etna released the new Lens, a crackle of lightning threading itself through the thrumming energy between them. More sweat slipped down his face as he focused all his energy on the Dark Oculator.

And then he dropped his gaze, looking down at himself for the smallest of moments, and then up at the Dark Oculator again.

Several things happened at once. Alcatraz cried out

in pain as the power from the Dark Oculator pushed through his focus. Etna cried out in pain as Alcatraz's Slantviewer's Lenses let Alcatraz channel her own gaze back at her—including all the Oculatory power she was currently forcing through it. An incredible amount of Oculatory power that rippled between them.

My skin began to feel like it was shrinking as the energy burned around me, and I stumbled backward, careful to avoid the edge of the platform. The remaining Librarians had retreated around the spire and out of sight, probably to keep themselves from being vaporized should the duel go wrong.

The energy between Alcatraz and Etna began to glow brighter and brighter as it traveled through the Slantviewer's Lens. Alcatraz screamed. Etna screamed.

And then the beams of energy between them exploded. For a terrifying second I could hear and see nothing, and felt only the now-familiar sensation of falling from an alarmingly high height as the shock wave propelled me off the top of the spire.

As my vision returned, I saw four things. First, the side of the Worldspire, shiny and crystalline and smooth as glass. Second, Alcatraz, falling not far from me. Third, the vast ocean below, rising to meet us at a speed at once too fast and too slow.

And finally, there at the tops
of the choppy, white-crested waves,
half a dozen fins circling.

Sharks.

"It had to be sharks!" Alcatraz screamed
at me.

"Do something, idiot!" I screamed back.
Alcatraz reached out with one hand and
grabbed my silver hair, using it to yank me
toward him.

"Ouch!" I yelled. "Not that!"

Alcatraz grabbed onto my arm, and then he
stretched out his other hand, still holding the
Slantviewer's Lenses, though his other two pairs
were nowhere to be seen. He twisted in the air,
rolling toward the tower until his arm knocked
against it.

And then, as suddenly as it had begun, the
falling stopped.

Let's talk for a minute about luck. Whenever you see someone who has something you want, like a sword or a cage in which to house all the Smedrys, you might think they are lucky. Sometimes this is accurate—they may have acquired that thing with no particular effort of their own. Other times, it might be because you, as an outsider, see only one small snapshot of that person's life. You don't see the training that was required for them to wield that sword effectively. You don't see the many years of carefully laid traps and plans required to trick all the Smedrys into a single cage at the same time.

In short, when you think someone else is lucky, you may be overlooking all the effort that went into getting where they are.

Luck, therefore, is a matter of perspective.

You might remember that in book one, I wanted to be Alcatraz. (You'd better remember. I explained that in *this* book, people.) I thought he was incredibly lucky to be an Oculator and a Smedry and have all the privileges and powers I wished I had. In some ways, it was true. Alcatraz hadn't done any work to achieve those things. He was born into them.

But he would rather have been a knight who could wield a sword.

Perspective is tricky that way.

So, while from my perspective what Alcatraz did when he touched the Worldspire might seem like luck, that luck is an illusion caused by the fact that I did not know what Alcatraz was thinking.

More on that in the next chapter.

Alcatraz and I stopped falling. We continued downward, but our speed slowed considerably as the air buffeted against us. The tops of the waves began to break off and float in midair like shiny amorphous blobs.

"What did you do?" I shouted at Alcatraz, though shouting was no longer quite as necessary, because the roar of the air in our ears quieted as we fell slower.

"I think . . ." Alcatraz said, "I think I broke gravity."

I looked up and found two Librarians floating above

us, others flying away from the tower at a wide angle. Bits and pieces of the glass dragon also hung in the air, flying out in all directions, but no longer plummeting toward the ground.

I stared at the Worldspire. I stared at the ocean, where globs were floating everywhere like shining confetti for as far as I could see, which from this height was a long, long way.

"*Everywhere?*" I asked. "You broke gravity *everywhere?*"

Alcatraz looked at me sheepishly.

You Hushlanders are probably doubting me now. Many of you are old enough to remember the time Alcatraz's Talent broke gravity across the entire world, and the fact that you don't seems like evidence that this never happened.

I will remind you that the Librarians have been lying to you and changing your memories for as long as you've been alive. You know that feeling you get when you realize you've been sitting in class, staring off into space, and you've lost track of time and have no memory of what happened around you?

Why do you think schools *have* Librarians anyway?

I twisted my arm in Alcatraz's and grabbed onto him, trying to pull him toward the spire. Maybe if we could grab onto it somehow, we could stop falling before we landed right on top of all those sharks.

"Um, Bastille?" Alcatraz said. He pointed the Slant-viewer's Lenses out across the water.

I looked past a flock of birds that flailed and twisted and squawked. Beyond them, in the distance, I saw something else spinning uncontrollably in the air.

The Gak. I wasn't sure if it had been swimming to-ward us, or had merely taken a leap on its island at ex-actly the wrong moment, but the Gak spun in gentle circles through the air, flailing its limbs and searching for anything at all to hang on to as bits of ocean water glittered around it.

This alone should have been enough to alarm me.

But it wasn't nearly as alarming as the thing ap-proaching us from below. A shark had angled itself up out of the water and was now careening toward us at roughly the same speed we were floating down toward it.

You Hushlanders learned from Newton that an object in motion wants to stay in motion, and an object at rest wants to stay at rest. You are wrong; objects aren't con-scious, and don't have the capability to want things. The only exceptions are talking rocks.

This shark, on the other hand, was quite conscious and looking at me with very definite desire.

"By the First Sands," I said. I looked around for something, anything, that was neither a shark nor a Librarian nor a glob of ocean water. A sparkling object flew parallel to us, a few yards past my right hand.

My sword.

"Alcatraz!" I shouted. "Help me get my sword!"

"You should see what you look like right now," Alcatraz responded. I glared at him. I knew what he meant—my hair was floating wildly around me like a great silver cloud. (Alcatraz's hair somehow always manages to float wildly, gravity or no gravity.)

I shoved Alcatraz away from me as hard as I possibly could. Alcatraz circled his arms, trying to reach for me, but it was too late. I was already flying away from him in the opposite direction.

Directly at my sword. I smiled and reached out and grabbed it.

And kept flying. I flailed in the air, I flipped a somersault, I turned a cartwheel, but without something to push against, I kept flying out over the ocean, away from the Worldspire, away from Alcatraz, away from the shark that was now going to pass squarely between us.

Until Alcatraz bounced off the Worldspire right into the path of the shark, which torpedoed toward him with its mouth open wide.

I wasn't about to throw my sword, but I did pass through a large glob of ocean water containing a small school of frantically spinning fish. My free hand closed around one of the fish, and I threw it away from the spire, which slowed my momentum somewhat. A few more thrown fish gave me just enough momentum to propel myself backward into a second, larger glob of water.

This one attached to a second, larger shark.

"Gak!" I shouted and wrapped my arms around the shark to keep it from twisting in the air. The shark writhed and snapped its teeth, sending saltwater globs flying into my hair, which at least wetted it enough that it began floating around my head in a more cohesive manner.

"Happy now, Alcatraz?" I shouted, before positioning myself on the correct side of the shark and shoving with the strength of several Crystin knights.

I was propelled toward Alcatraz, who was just now coming head-to-head—literally—with the open-mouthed shark. I twisted in the air, leading with my sword and aiming my blade downward.

And then we all collided: Alcatraz, the gaping-mawed shark, and me.

Chapter
· 13 ·

Back on the subject of perspective. I want you to remember that I did not know what Alcatraz was thinking. At the time, I did not know he'd had what amounted to a falling-out with his Talent in the last book, or that it abandoned him because he insisted on blaming it for everything wrong in the world when it was only trying to help.

This is what's called *point of view*—that thing I violated back in Chapter Eight by telling you what Alcatraz was thinking. Now you might say I've violated your trust by *not* telling you what Alcatraz was thinking before he broke gravity and saved us from falling into the ocean.

To which I say, here's my literary license. Try to take it away from me.

As we collided with the shark, my sword slipped right between its open teeth and pierced through the top of its head. The shark writhed on the end of my sword as the three of us floated next to the spire.

I'd had enough of this. We were much nearer the surface of the ocean than we were the top of the tower, and as far as I could tell, there were no more Librarians up there to fight. Not at this moment anyway.

All I wanted was to get my feet on some solid ground. Preferably with Grappler's Glass to hold me there, but a girl has to take what she can get.

I withdrew my sword from the head and threw the shark up and to the side, propelling us with equal force toward the base of the spire. I missed, unfortunately, and we splashed into the ocean, sending the water flying in little globs up into the air as we more or less bounced off and began to ascend again.

This time though, we were close enough to the platform around the bottom of the spire that I could grab onto one of the pillars that lined the edges. I snatched Alcatraz by the hair with one hand (payback is sweet) and hooked my feet around the pillar with the other. Then I slowly climbed down, dragging Alcatraz and my sword with me as I went.

"Well," I said when we reached the bottom of the pillar, "how are we going to fix *this*?"

Alcatraz locked his ankles around the pillar next to me and reached out to poke a finger into a bit of water as it floated by. "I don't know," he said.

"Your Talent worked again though," I said. "We were falling, and it saved us."

Alcatraz nodded. "I think it had something to do with the spire."

I squinted at him. "How did you know that would work?"

Alcatraz squirmed. "I could see my Talent. Or a reflection of it, I guess, in the crystal surface."

I gaped at him. "You *saw* your Talent? What did it look like?"

"Angry," Alcatraz said. "I think—I think it's mad at me."

"How can a Talent be mad at you?" I asked. "It's not a person. It's barely even a thing."

Alcatraz let go of his Slantviewer's Lenses, and they hung in the air beside him. I reached out and grabbed them before they could float away. I felt a slight hum as I touched them.

And, ever so slightly, the Lenses began to glow.

"Bastille," Alcatraz said, "what did you—"

"Nothing," I snapped, handing the glasses to him. "I'm not an Oculator."

I'd wanted to be an Oculator my whole life, but here's the thing about luck: just as Alcatraz could never train and work hard enough to become a Knight of Crystallia, I would never be able to work hard enough to become an Oculator. While you can work for some things, others are governed *only* by luck. There was no reason to imagine that could be changed. "Besides, we're talking about you and your angry Talent. Why is it mad at you anyway?"

"The power of the Incarna is building up now that the Talents aren't releasing the pressure a bit at a time," Alcatraz said. "And it's done strange things to *my* Oculatory abilities, so maybe you—"

"*No,*" I said.

Alcatraz extended the Lenses to me. "Take off your Warrior's Lenses and put them on."

"Shut up or I'll throw them in the ocean," I said.

"Bastille—"

Let me be clear that I knew Alcatraz was about to argue with me that I was being stupid, that I had seen and done some pretty incredible things since waking up in the Highbrary, and I shouldn't rule out that being an Oculator was one of those things.

Instead, midsentence, Alcatraz's demeanor changed entirely. His eyes narrowed. He stared right at me and said, "You again. This is all *your* fault."

I felt like he'd stabbed me with my own sword. "What?" I said. "*I'm* not the one who—"

"Not *you*," Alcatraz said, grabbing my Warrior's Lenses right off my face. He held them in front of him, staring at his own reflection.

Shattering Glass. We were not going through *that* again. "Look," I said. "I don't see what difference it makes whose fault it is. I—"

"What?" Alcatraz yelled, dropping the Slantviewer's Lenses. "You think you can just abandon me and then pop back up in my life and destroy *gravity*? Where have you *been* anyway?"

I stared at Alcatraz. He stared at his reflection. The Slantviewer's Lenses floated in the air between us. I reached out and took them again, so they wouldn't float away, and when I did, they began to hum once more.

"Alcatraz," I said, but he was too busy staring at his own reflection in the Warrior's Lenses.

At this point, I had two choices. I could convince myself that both Alcatraz and I had lost our minds, and perhaps were actually drowning in the ocean right now rather than clinging to the base of the Worldspire.

Or I could admit that something very strange was going on with Alcatraz and his Talent, and me and his Lenses.

I really didn't want to have lost my mind. I'm rather partial to it. So instead I took a deep breath, put on the Slantviewer's Lenses, looked at Alcatraz, and tapped them.

I could feel the power in them even before I looked at the Warrior's Lenses and tapped them again.

My vision shifted so abruptly that I hugged the pillar to stay upright. Staring through the Lenses at Alcatraz's reflection, I could see the Warrior's Lenses as if they were held in my own hands, exactly as Alcatraz saw them. But the reflection—it was no longer Alcatraz. It *looked* like him, but the eyes were darker, meaner, his whole demeanor sullen and angry. Kind of like Alcatraz that time I took pictures of him wearing a tunic.

In my shock, I nearly forgot I was currently wearing and using Lenses that were generally restricted to Oculators. "What is that?" I asked.

"My Talent," Alcatraz said. "The thing that destroyed everything."

"But it didn't," I said. "You said the Talents were siphoning off the energy of the Incarna. They're what's kept all of us from burning up, right? It was only trying to help."

Alcatraz stared at the reflection, and the reflection stared angrily back.

"We need to bring back the Talents," I said to Alcatraz. "Biblioden hasn't arrived yet. If you had your Talent, you'd be better able to fight against him. And if the others had theirs, they might be able to—"

"It abandoned me," Alcatraz said. "If I hadn't—if I hadn't broken the Talents, then my grandfather would have arrived late to the bullet. He would still be alive. I could have broken that altar, or the power that Biblioden used to make the bloodforged Lens from my father's soul. I hate my Talent. It's what caused all of this."

"That doesn't make any sense, Alcatraz," I said. "Either it could have saved your grandfather and it abandoned you when you needed it, or it's a terrible thing that has always ruined your life. But it can't be both."

(This is not true, of course. Something can be both the bane of your existence and your favorite thing in the world. Just look at my relationship with Al.)

The Talent shook its head at us. It pointed right at Alcatraz, and its mouth began to move.

You hate me, the Talent said. I couldn't hear the words, but I could understand them, maybe because I was seeing the Talent as Alcatraz did through the Lenses, and he knew perfectly well what it was saying.

"You didn't help!" Alcatraz screamed. "My grandfather died and so did my father, and you didn't do anything!"

The Talent pointed out at the ocean, as if to say, *Yes, but you didn't get eaten by sharks.*

"It's right, Alcatraz," I said. "We didn't die by plummeting into the ocean, and we didn't get eaten alive. We got to the Worldspire, even though we shouldn't have been able to reach it before Biblioden did. It saved us. Twice." And a lot more times than that, before I went into the coma.

The Talent nodded, gesturing to the side as if to say, *Yeah, listen to her.*

Alcatraz shook his head. "I don't know how to fix gravity," he said miserably. "I don't know how to bring the Talents back. I don't fix things. I only break them."

For a moment, the three of us simply looked at each other.

"Maybe," I said to Alcatraz, "you should start by saying you're sorry."

Alcatraz turned and glared at me. I could see him out of the sides of my Lenses.

"What?" I said. "Would it kill you to try?"

"Because *you're* so good at apologizing," Alcatraz muttered.

"I am *great* at apologizing," I said. "I'm even better at never needing to."

"I'm not going to apologize to my Talent," Alcatraz said.

The Talent rolled its eyes, folded its arms, and began to brood like a sparkly vampire.

"Fine," I said. "We'll just hang out here until Biblioden figures out how to fly his ship without gravity, and then we'll face him with nothing but my sword and a pair of Slantviewer's Lenses, instead of having help from the Breaking Talent, the most powerful Talent the world has ever known. Sounds great. I bet the ending of this book is going to be even better than the last one."

Hooray for irony.

Alcatraz hung his head, a mirror of his own reflection. I was trying to figure out where to put my sword to free up my punching hand, when Alcatraz blurted out, "I'm sorry."

The Talent's head snapped up.

"I'm sorry I blamed you," Alcatraz said. "I used to feel like the need to break things built up in me over time, and if I didn't let it out, I would break bigger, more important things. More impressively, more destructively, more and more, and I couldn't make it stop. But you were doing what Alcatraz the First made you for. You were trying to send that energy somewhere, so that all the Free King-domers could live. And over time, I figured out how to direct the energy. I figured out how to break things for the greater good." Alcatraz shook his head. "Without you, I'm nothing. I failed to stop Biblioden from killing my father. I'm a coward, and I know that's why you left me."

"That's not true," I said. "You're a hero, even without the Talent."

"No," Alcatraz said. "I'm a failure. I'm sorry, Bastille. I'm sorry I didn't recognize the Talents for what they were, and I'm sorry I can't use them now."

Alcatraz closed his eyes.

And the Talent smiled.

"Hey," I said. "I think it worked!"

"Ouch!" Alcatraz shouted as we both fell on our be-hinds onto the wooden steps at the bottom of the World-spire. All around us, great globs of ocean and fish and kelp and sharks went splashing down, followed by bits of glass from the *Dragonaut* and parts of the Librarian blimp. The pillar Alcatraz was holding fractured, and I barely rolled out of the way as the rubble crumbled around us, shards of it scattering into the sea, where the waves slowly began to form normally again.

"You broke the pillar!" I shouted. "You have your Talent back!"

Alcatraz unburied himself from the pillar's rubble, looking both shocked and unsure. I thrust the Slantviewer's Lenses at him, and he tucked them into his pocket.

"I have my Talent back," Alcatraz said. "The Talents . . . are they all fixed?"

We waited, as if for a sign. Which was stupid, because Alcatraz was the only Smedry present, and it wasn't as if *I* was suddenly going to develop a Smedry Talent. For a moment, nothing happened.

And then we heard footsteps approach us.

"Alcatraz!" Kaz yelled, and both Alcatraz and I turned to see him running toward us. "You did it! You fixed the Talents! I was so surprised when I got lost just now. And arrived here so quickly! My Talent is being even more cooperative than usual!"

Alcatraz looked uncertain for a moment, and then he smiled. "Thanks," he said to my Warrior's Lenses.

"Kaz!" I said. "Where are Folsom and Himalaya and my mother?"

"We escaped to a safe house!" Kaz called. "They're quite all right. But I have even better news. Guess who I found on the way here?"

"Leaping Levines, boy!" Alcatraz and I were both startled to see Grandpa Smedry himself running toward us from behind Kaz, grinning from ear to ear. "You did it!"

"Grandpa?" Alcatraz said. "I thought you were—"

"Dead?" Leavenworth exclaimed. He had an oversized hunk of gauze duct-taped to the bridge of his nose, and he seemed to be having a hard time seeing around it. Kaz grabbed him by the elbow to keep him from stumbling off into the ocean. "Wrestling Wredes, it will take a lot more than this bullet to kill me. Now where's your father, Alcatraz? Were you able to stop Biblioden?"

Kaz's face fell. Alcatraz took a step back, bits of crystal pillar crumbling under his shoes.

Leavenworth looked at him with a big, happy smile, with no idea what news he was about to receive.

Chapter

14

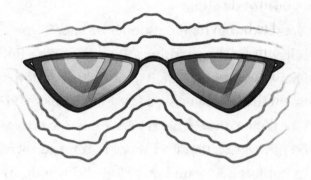

It has been brought to my attention that because some of you didn't find the note I left at the end of the fifth volume of this series, you aren't fully aware of what happened to Leavenworth. For those of you who may have missed it, let me fill you in. Leavenworth, while no one knew it, did manage to call out to his broken Talent before the bullet reached his brain. Because of desperation, and loyalty, and magic and stuff.

Oh, forget it. I'm going to let him tell it.

"Grandpa," Alcatraz said, "how did you survive?" Alcatraz looked like he was caught between disbelief (that his grandfather was alive), pure joy (that his grandfather was alive), and horror (at the news he was about to tell him). He was obviously trying to put off telling his grandfather the truth, but many of you have the same question about Leavenworth's survival, so for the moment your needs align.

It was bound to happen sooner or later.

"Talents are slippery things," Leavenworth said. "You may have broken it, but it couldn't abandon me at a moment like that. I arrived late to the bullet and came to on the floor of the Highbrary just in time to arrive late to a flood of magma, though I was still trapped there until Kazan got lost and found me. How did you do it? How did you fix the Talents?"

"I, um," Alcatraz said. "I apologized to them."

"Persnickety Pierces, boy!" Leavenworth said. "Nothing fixes broken things like a good apology. Well done, boy. Well done indeed!"

"It must have been an impressive apology," Kaz said. "One step and I was there with my father, and another step and we were both here. Maybe you should apologize more often."

"No," Alcatraz said, and both Leavenworth and Kaz looked at him in surprise. Alcatraz appeared to choke on his own words, and then shook his head and started again. "No, Grandpa, I didn't do well. I failed. We didn't stop Biblioden. He killed my father, and used him to make a bloodforged Lens to channel the power of the Incarna into everyone in the Free Kingdoms, to burn them up. And I don't know how to stop it."

Leavenworth blinked, taking that in. He'd been worried before that Attica might have perished, but he'd never been confronted so squarely with the certainty of his son's death.

Kaz looked down at his feet, almost as if he felt guilty for not having broken the news himself, though he'd only been with Leavenworth a few seconds longer than we had.

"No, boy," Leavenworth said finally. "You didn't fail. There's nothing you could have done to stop him from killing your father."

Alcatraz pressed his lips together. "Biblioden gave me a choice. He said I could choose who he killed, and I chose Dad. It's my fault he's dead."

Leavenworth shook his head again. "My boy—"

"No!" Alcatraz shouted at him. "Don't tell me it's not my fault! You weren't there, Grandpa. You didn't watch him die."

"That's true, lad," Leavenworth said. As he spoke, I could see Alcatraz's shoulders hunching, his eyebrows drawing together, his eyes narrowing like the image of the Talent.

Leavenworth meant well, but he was undoing all the progress Alcatraz had made.

"And I'm sorry you had to be there to see that," Leavenworth went on, "but—"

"Smedrys!" I shouted. All three of them looked at me in surprise, which gave me a second to collect myself, because I hadn't thought much past yelling that first word. "This sentimentality will have to be postponed," I snapped. "Preferably indefinitely, but at least until after we get to the top of the spire and stop Biblioden from destroying us all. Mmkay?"

"Bastille," Leavenworth said. "I think Alcatraz needs—"

"She's right," Alcatraz said. "You all need to save the world, and I'm only getting in the way."

"No!" I shouted at Alcatraz. "You are going to help us save the world, if I have to drag you by your ear!"

Alcatraz's hands went instinctively to his ears, probably because I'd done that, quite literally, in Chapter Five. Alcatraz turned, his wrath now focused on me.

"Shut up, Bastille," he said. "You weren't there either. You don't know what it was like."

I don't know if it was Alcatraz's words or his Talent that did it, but at that moment, something inside of me broke. Not my patience, as I had already lost that in Chapter Eight. No, what broke was my bravado, the façade I used to keep myself from crumbling while there was still a world to save.

Alcatraz was right. I *wasn't* there, and I'm his shattering Crystin knight, and I *should* have been.

Whatever Alcatraz saw on my face at that moment, it was enough to give him pause. His anger faded slightly, and he opened his mouth, probably to say something else irrevocably hurtful and stoopid.

So I did the only thing I could think of. I punched him.

"Ow!" Alcatraz yelled, holding his shoulder where I'd given him a solid wallop. "That hurt!"

"So did what you said, you idiot!" I yelled at him.

"Bastille," Leavenworth tried to cut in, "Alcatraz, I don't think—"

"Fine!" Alcatraz shouted. "I'm done talking about my father, and I'm done talking about my feelings, and I'm done trying to save the stupid world when I'm clearly not the one it wants to save it!"

And then he stalked off around the spire in the direction Kaz and Leavenworth had come from.

Chapter

15

I'm not going to write a chapter introduction here. If you want one, too bad. Helping you understand the intricacies of human emotion is not nearly as important as taking care of my friend, who had just stormed off. I wasn't about to let Alcatraz wander off alone and get eaten by a stray shark.

"Bastille," Leavenworth said as I moved to follow after Alcatraz, "perhaps we should give him a moment."

"We don't have a moment!" I snapped at him. "We got here ahead of Biblioden, but we don't know by how much, so we need to prepare to stop him. So why don't you two get lost and come back with something useful for once!"

I stalked after Alcatraz before Kaz could object that he *had*, the moment he got his Talent back. I was in no mood to argue. And I wasn't going to give Alcatraz any more moments to wallow in his misery and self-loathing. He'd had enough.

I found Alcatraz slumped on the platform between the spire and the sea, next to several broken shards of a potted plant that must have gotten overturned when gravity broke. Down the way, I could see the edge of the small city at the base of the spire, where researchers lived while they studied the tower. The buildings looked mostly intact, though the platform around them was littered with overturned vehicles, a few flopping fish, and several very disoriented-looking birds.

"Go away, Bastille!" Alcatraz yelled.

"No," I told him. "I will not go away until you admit that what happened to your father isn't your fault."

"That's not going to happen," Alcatraz said.

"Why not?" I asked.

"Because it *is* my fault."

"No it isn't!"

Alcatraz climbed to his feet and faced me as I reached him, still hauling along my sword. I had half a mind to hit him with *it* this time, instead of my fist. "Why not?"

"Because!" I yelled, right in his face. "It's *MINE*."

Alcatraz stuttered. "W-what?"

"It's *MY FAULT!*" I shouted at him.

"Bastille," he said, "you were in a coma."

"Which I *wouldn't* have been if I hadn't taken that incredible risk in the battle in Mokia," I said. "It's my job to protect you Smedrys. Whose job was it to keep Attica alive? Not yours. Smedrys cause problems and get themselves into danger, and Knights of Crystallia keep them from getting their stupid selves killed. That's how it works, Alcatraz." I switched my sword to my off hand and punched him in the arm again.

I expected him to yell at me, tell me I was wrong, but instead he merely winced and cradled his arm.

"So, you were right!" I shouted, punching him again. "I wasn't there! I should have been there to keep Leavenworth from getting shot. I should have been there to keep you from getting tied to that altar. I should have been there to keep Attica from dying. You didn't fail, Alcatraz. *I DID!*"

"Bastille!" Alcatraz yelled, and though I was pretty sure I'd punched him hard enough to seriously hurt him, Alcatraz reached out and put a hand on each of my arms.

Probably to keep me from punching him again, now that I consider it. At the time, all I could think about was how close Alcatraz's face was, his eyes staring into mine. I felt a flush climb slowly up my body and settle in my cheeks. I tried to pull away, but Alcatraz held on tight.

"Bastille," he said, "you didn't fail. You're the only reason we've gotten this far."

Now *he* was looking at me with concern. I meant to shout at him to leave me alone, to break away and stalk off the way he did to me, but instead I did something very, very stoopid.

(Yes, Alcatraz. I admit that it happens. I probably should have set that last paragraph apart on its own page, because Alcatraz is going to want to frame it. But I don't like to make things easy for him.)

I kissed him.

Alcatraz's lips went soft in surprise. I took a step back in horror, and we stared at each other. My skin burned from head to toe, and Alcatraz's face turned a deep shade of crimson.

I turned on my heels and ran.

* * *

When I returned to the spot where I'd left Kaz and Leavenworth, they were gone. Lost, probably. I hoped they made it count, because we were still at the bottom of the enormous Worldspire with only two pairs of Lenses, my sword, and the Breaking Talent. I scanned the skies, but there was still no sign of Biblioden. I set down my sword, curled my arms around my knees, and glared at the ocean.

BASTILLE WOULD NEVER ADMIT IT, BUT I SAW HER. SHE CRIED.
—ALCATRAZ

This was not the first time I'd failed as a knight, but it was definitely the first time I felt I'd failed as a person. The Smedrys weren't just my responsibility; they were my friends. When they weren't driving me crazy, I truly cared about them.

(Okay, maybe I still care about them when they are driving me crazy. Which is good for them, because that's most of the time.)

What I'd said to Alcatraz was true. I should have been there to save Leavenworth from the bullet that will someday reach his brain. I should have been there to save Attica from dying on that altar of outdated encyclopedias. But most of all, I should have been there to protect Alcatraz from ever having to answer Biblioden's stupid question about who should die. From having to face that all alone. I felt more than guilty—I felt ashamed.

And now I'd gone and *kissed* him, and he was going to think I had all kinds of mushy *feelings* for him. Even worse, I *did* have mushy feelings. There, I said it. Are you happy now?

And okay, fine. I cried. Daintily and with a quiet inner strength.

Challenge me on that, Al, I dare you.

As I sat there, I did the same thing Alcatraz had been doing—I leaned into arrogance and took credit for things beyond my control. There is one simple reason why.

Arrogance is easier. Arrogance is safer. Because if the terrible thing that happened is all your fault, there's still the chance that you'll be able to stop future terrible things from happening.

Sometimes blaming yourself feels better than admitting that the fate of the world may be out of your control.

When Alcatraz approached, he did so slowly, with great trepidation. Which was probably smart, since I still had a big crystal sword.

I didn't look at him. I couldn't. I'd made a complete fool out of myself, and (*maybe*) worse, I'd failed him.

Alcatraz sat down beside me and sighed. "It's not your fault, Bastille," he said. After a long moment he added, "And it's not mine either."

I sniffled. With obvious inner strength. Happy as I was that he was finally willing to admit that, I didn't know what to say. I'd kissed him. My lips touched his lips. My cheeks felt like a baledragon had taken up residence in my face.

And then Alcatraz reached over and took my hand in his. His skin was soft and warm, and his fingers curled naturally against mine.

He stole a glance at me at the same time I stole a glance at him, and his cheeks were still as bright a red as I'm sure mine were.

"Idiot," I said to him.

But I didn't let go of his hand.

Chapter

16

All right. Enough mushy stuff. Fortunately, Biblioden showed up a few minutes later and interrupted us before we got any more quivery and unsympathetic.

This isn't a romance novel, after all.

"Look!" Alcatraz said, pointing up at the sky.

I didn't have to look. I'd already seen the big glass blimp flying toward the Worldspire at an alarming speed. It was definitely Librarian.

"Where did my grandfather go?" Alcatraz asked, dropping my hand and glancing around like it only now occurred to him that there had been two other Smedrys here when he ran off.

"He got lost," I said. "I think."

Alcatraz looked over at the staircase that wound up the side of the spire. "Bastille," he said, "how are we going to get—"

"Idiot," I said to him. "Hop on."

So there I was, racing up the stairs of the Worldspire with Alcatraz riding on my back, my sword held in one hand. I ducked close to the spire, trying to stay out of sight of the blimp as it landed far above us on the platform we'd flown off of during the explosion.

You might think I was upset to have to climb stairs high into the atmosphere with Alcatraz on my back, but in truth I was elated. We were already one step ahead of Biblioden, having destroyed or otherwise scattered the crew of Librarians who were supposed to prepare the way for him. I had my sword, and Alcatraz had his Talent. Kaz's Talent was being more helpful than ever and had already been deployed on our behalf.

I was ready to confront Biblioden and his cult of Librarians with all the fury of the Smedry family and the Knights of Crystallia.

But first we had to get, well, *up there.*

I drew on the power of the other knights, summoning their endurance as I charged up the stairs. My legs moved faster than they ever could have without the help of the Mindstone, and my muscles miraculously didn't tire. We wound up and up the staircase for miles at top speed, Alcatraz clinging to my shoulders and making little terrified squealing noises whenever we got too close to the edge.

"Shut up, you big baby," I told him.

"I don't want to have to break gravity again," Alcatraz said.

That was fair. Though having an army of sharks to fling at Biblioden would add to our assets nicely.

I looked down—just for a moment—and accidentally veered a bit too close to the edge. We were barely halfway up the spire, and already the ocean seemed a terribly long way down. The waves frothed and churned as out of them emerged the bulbous body of—was that the Gak? I supposed it had to have gone *somewhere* after we got gravity back. If it was tossing around in the ocean at the base of the spire, at least it wasn't waiting for us at the top.

"Bastille," Alcatraz said, "did you see—"

"Hush," I said. "I don't want them to hear us coming."

That, as it turned out, was unavoidable. My boots pounded against the stairs until we reached the platform at the top, where a group of Librarians was waiting for us.

Beyond them, another Librarian in a thick robe ascended the stairs toward the tip of the spire.

It was strange to see him standing there, looking just

like Alcatraz's cousin Dif, whom I'd had the misfortune of meeting once or twice. I recognized his wild, curly hair, and the beard that grew along his chin. At least he'd gotten rid of the terrible plaids he usually wore. Though this probably wasn't what the real Dif had looked like at all, since Biblioden had found and killed him when he was a child under deep cover in the Hushlands with his parents.

It burned that he'd been among us all along. I'd *protected* Dif once, when he was on a mission in the Hushlands with Leavenworth. And all that time he had been Biblioden the Scrivener, lurking among the Smedrys, waiting for his chance to destroy us all.

Biblioden circled the spire, something the size of a Lens glinting in his hand.

"He has the bloodforged Lens!" Alcatraz shouted. "We have to get to him."

That wasn't a problem. While some of the Librarians in our way had guns, none of them had Alcatraz riding on their back. I'd like to see them try to hurt me without their various weapons splintering and breaking.

I got a running start and began bobbing and weaving through the Librarians, making straight for the stairs to the spire's tip in the center of the platform. Guns and swords broke with snaps and pops and twangs to our

left and right as we passed. Biblioden reached the crow's nest at the top, disappearing momentarily from sight.

"Bastille, look out!" Alcatraz shouted, and I leaped out from under a cudgel wielded by a muscled Librarian who was almost as large as Alcatraz's cousin Sing Smedry. The cudgel was a good idea—it was far more technologically advanced than the swords or the guns, and therefore less susceptible to Smedry Talents. We had nearly reached the stairs, and I prepared to make one last great Mindstone-augmented leap toward the landing.

"Biblioden is doing something up there," Alcatraz said. "I can feel the power. What is he—"

And then, suddenly, one of the Librarians tripped.

It wasn't an ordinary stumble or snag across the crystalline surface of the tower. The Librarian in question flew out in front of me, landing face-first on the ground in a place I very much did not expect her to be the moment before. I dodged, but this trip was so timely and skillful that even my Crystin reflexes couldn't avoid it. I stumbled over the Librarian, and Alcatraz tumbled from my back. A terrible thought rang through my mind.

That Librarian somehow had the Talent to trip over nothing at all.

Even armed with that knowledge, nothing could have prepared me for what happened next. Somewhere farther back in the crowd, a Librarian began to sing terribly. The cacophony sounded like an elephant with a head cold was stepping on a flock of angry geese. And then, without warning, the entire line of Librarians I had been about to jump over began to dance extremely poorly. Their feet went one direction while their arms went another, and their hips gyrated somewhere in between. I shouted for Alcatraz and positioned myself between the line of dancing Librarians and where I hoped Alcatraz was, though I didn't dare turn around to look for him. Not with the threat we were currently facing.

"Biblioden!" I shouted. "He—"

"He reached the spire, and he used that Lens to give them all Smedry Talents!" Alcatraz called back.

Was this what Biblioden made the bloodforged Lens for? To create an army as powerful as the Smedry family?

And *then* to vaporize everyone who challenged him? That couldn't be right. It didn't make sense.

"Bastille!" Alcatraz called. "You have to get out of there!"

"Not a chance," I said, readying my sword as the line of dancing Librarians approached—elbows and knees jerking in all directions like some kind of cross between tai chi and the chicken dance. I'd spent my life defending Smedrys. I'd run afoul of all their Talents at one time or another—and that was with them on *my* side. The number of nights I'd fallen asleep thinking of all the ways I'd like to turn their Talents against them—well, it was far too many to count.

I'd spent my entire life preparing for this. I was going to destroy these Librarians before they knew what hit them.

I kept half an eye on my flank. Sure enough, a few of the Librarians behind the conga line charged forward and got lost, finding themselves conveniently behind me. I executed a perfect spin, taking them out while still keeping the advancing line in front of me.

And then I had an idea. "Hey!" I shouted at the crowd of Librarians. "How much rope do I have?"

Off to the side, a Librarian who had just become tragically bad at math shouted, "Zero feet plus zero inches divided by seventy-two times one thousand equals . . ."

"Well?" I demanded. The dancing Librarians were almost upon me, and I didn't think my sword was going to protect me from them. Hopefully none of them had the Breaking Talent, since it was rare. But even so, I'd seen what Folsom and Himalaya were capable of when they really got dancing.

"Forty-seven feet!" the Librarian shouted.

I smiled as the rope appeared, hanging off my elbow in a perfect loop.

"Thanks!" I said. I let out a length of rope, tied it into a lasso, and hooked it around the shimmying form of the Librarian at the end of the line. With a burst of Crystin speed, I ran to the other end of the line and then leaped behind them and across their flank, encircling them in the rope, and pulled tight. The badly dancing Librarians tripped over each other, landing in a huge tangle.

"Get to Biblioden!" I yelled at Alcatraz, not taking the time to see if he followed my instructions. Another squad of Librarians advanced on me, guns at the ready, when one of their guns spontaneously fell to pieces, metal bits clanging to the ground.

Oh no. One of them *did* have the Breaking Talent. While they all wore nearly identical robes, this Librarian had a long blond braid wound about her head—I was going to need to keep my eye on her, since she was one of the most dangerous.

The Librarian at the front suddenly started patting his pockets, searching for the gun he'd been holding a moment before. I smiled. The Losing Talent. Excellent.

"Where are your friends?" I shouted at him.

The Librarian turned around, but his entire squad

was gone. Lost. I cut down the Losing Librarian before he could go and lose *me*.

A Librarian with a sword advanced on me, but she sneezed at an inappropriate moment, closing her eyes. I dodged to avoid being blinded by a volley of snot, and then dispatched her as well.

Where was Alcatraz? I didn't love the idea of making him face Biblioden alone, which meant I needed to get up the stairs. These Librarians clearly weren't very adept at using their Talents, lacking the combined experience of the Smedry clan. Besides that, I liked to think that in the war between the Free Kingdoms and the Librarians, the Talents were on *our* side.

That didn't stop the Librarian who was bad at math from calling from the sidelines. "She's taken down twenty-three of our people, and we brought forty-seven, which means we still have . . ."

Oh no.

"Eighty-nine Librarians left to fight!"

I supposed that number could have been worse.

More Librarians appeared, seemingly out of nowhere. I swung my sword at the nearest one. The blow connected, but the Librarian didn't appear fazed.

Shattering Glass. She was arriving late to the blow.

That was almost as dangerous as the Breaking Talent, and I wasn't sure where the Breaking Librarian had gone. Theoretically she'd gotten lost with the rest of her squad, but with a Talent like that, I doubted she'd stay that way.

I backed away, moving swiftly toward the edge of the platform. The Librarian with the Talent for arriving late followed, still not showing any signs of pain. When I got near the edge I swung again, connecting once more, but with no effect.

The Librarian launched herself at me. I dodged and gave her a push, shoving her right over the edge.

She went hurtling toward the ocean below. With a Talent that powerful, I didn't believe for a second this was going to kill her. She'd arrive late to the fall, no doubt.

But at least that should take her a while.

When I turned around, I found the Librarian with the winding blond braids standing immediately behind me. She smiled as the platform began to crumble below our feet.

I moved around her as fast as I could, hoping she'd fall with the bits of tower, but she stepped back as well, maintaining her balance. Bits of crystal sloughed off. This tower was supposed to be connected to every living person in the world, and I wondered what kind of head-ache the whole of humanity was going to have after *that*.

It didn't matter. What mattered now was reaching Biblioden and stopping him from killing us all.

But first I had to deal with this Librarian. The Break-ing Talent was too powerful to ignore. I didn't dare use my sword against such a power, but I could turn it to my advantage. I dodged between Librarians, launching a few of them at the Breaking Librarian. One broke their sword, and another their leg. In the process, the Librar-ian with the braids also unraveled the sleeves of her own robes to the shoulder.

What can I say? That Talent is weird.

The Librarian with the braids advanced on me. "Is that the best you can do, Crystin?" she asked.

"I don't know," I said to a nearby Librarian I'd heard mumbling to himself. "What do you think?"

"I think her bottom is showing," said the Librarian with an obvious Talent for saying awkward things at in-appropriate times.

The braided Librarian's eyes widened, and her hands reached around to the back of her robe—now disinte-grated along with her sleeves—and she yelped. I picked up the Awkward Librarian and threw him at her, pitching her over the edge of the tower while she was caught off guard.

I'm guessing she broke his fall.

I would have done some victory dancing (probably poorly; I've never been much of a dancer), were it not for the gibberish shouted by a Librarian near the center of the platform. "Slipping and sliding, dishes make waves!" the Librarian said.

Dishes make waves.

Oh. Oh no. Oh no no no.

Libby Smedry had a Talent for spilling copious amounts of water on the floor while washing the dishes. I was pretty sure that required *actual* dishes though—

"Zero dishes divided by fifty-eight Librarians to the third power makes seven dishes each!" the math-impaired Librarian shouted.

Shattering Glass. The Librarians were all suddenly carrying seven dishes each. I looked frantically around for whichever one was going to try to wash them—

But my eyes caught on Alcatraz. He was hiding behind the stairs leading up the spire instead of following Biblioden. But he didn't look like he was wallowing again. Instead he had his eyes closed, like he was focusing on something.

"Alcatraz!" I shouted. "What are you—"

And then a Librarian came running down the stairs, spat on his sleeve, and rubbed one of his dishes with the cuff.

From behind the tip of the spire came the biggest wave of water I had ever seen.

So much for the Talents being on our side. "Alcatraz!" I shouted. "Take cover!" I grabbed onto the only thing I could find—the end of the rope I'd used to lasso the mass of still-dancing Librarians.

The water crashed across the ledge, sending Librarians sliding along the surface with it. I pulled myself toward the center of the platform, hoping the wave wouldn't have the force to wash me over the edge, but the water swept my feet out from under me. I clung to the rope with one hand and the hilt of my sword with the other, swimming against the current, but to no avail.

What? *You* try swimming into a tidal wave with both hands full sometime and see how far *you* get.

The wave washed me over the edge of the platform, and once again I began to plummet. I tightened my grip on the rope, hoping that the bunch of dancing Librarians still tangled in it would be heavy enough not to be washed over the edge along with me.

My ears popped just then, and a second later I felt a force travel through my chest, like I'd been hit by a sound wave or a sudden blast of pressure. Which Talent was that? I didn't remember anything like it. It couldn't be a new one, could it?

The water drained off the platform above, raining around me, further drenching my armor and my hair. (Again.) I couldn't climb the rope without letting go of my sword, so I just squeezed tight.

There was an eerie silence, and then Alcatraz appeared at the top of the rope. "Hang on!" he shouted, as if I were about to do anything else.

He began pulling on the rope, hoisting me up to the top. When he got me high enough to grab my wrist, I slung my foot on top of the ledge and scrambled up. There were still a few dozen Librarians up here. The mass in the tangle of rope had stopped dancing, and were rapidly freeing themselves and drawing what was left of their swords and handguns.

"What was that?" I asked. "Did Biblioden finish his ritual? But we're still—"

"It wasn't Biblioden," Alcatraz said. "I—I broke their Talents."

I smiled. Of course he did. The only thing more dangerous than a bunch of Talents is a Smedry who knows how to use one. "Well done," I said.

Alcatraz shook his head at me. "You were amazing."

"Yeah, well," I said to him, "I've had a lot of time to think about what I'd like to do with you Smedrys and your shattering Talents."

Alcatraz's eyes widened, like he'd always known I was restraining myself, but he hadn't ever quite grasped the details of *what* I was holding back.

I might have laughed, but at that moment I noticed what the mess of Talents had left us. There were now at least five times as many Librarians as there had been before. They may have lost their Talents, but they still had the resources their Talents had provided them— including an alarming number of cudgels and dishes and other objects that were more technologically developed and therefore less vulnerable to the Breaking Talent.

They advanced, moving between us and the stairs, spreading out so that even with Crystin speed I wasn't sure I could dodge through them. Meanwhile, Biblioden was still up at the top of the spire, no doubt preparing to vaporize us all.

We had to get up there, but I wasn't sure we could do it alone.

"What do we do?" Alcatraz asked. "Surrender?"

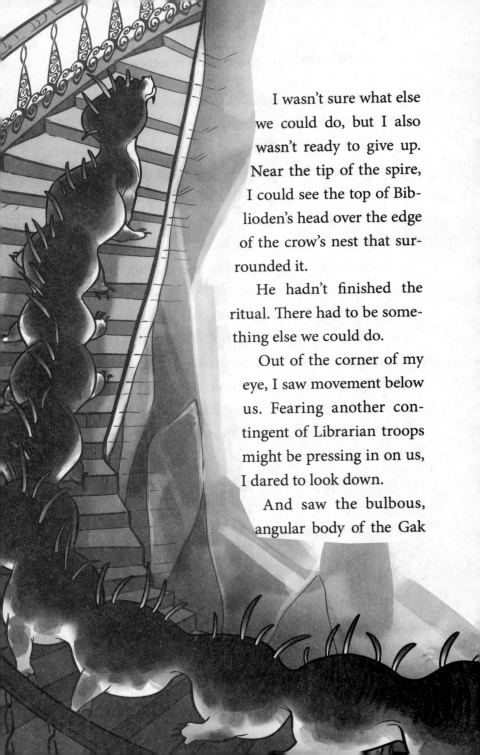

I wasn't sure what else we could do, but I also wasn't ready to give up. Near the tip of the spire, I could see the top of Biblioden's head over the edge of the crow's nest that surrounded it.

He hadn't finished the ritual. There had to be something else we could do.

Out of the corner of my eye, I saw movement below us. Fearing another contingent of Librarian troops might be pressing in on us, I dared to look down.

And saw the bulbous, angular body of the Gak

slithering up the staircase that threaded up the side of the tower. If we didn't do something, we would be sandwiched between the army of Librarians and the Gak when it reached the landing, and it would surely still be looking to eat us.

Though if we played it right, *that* would make a good distraction.

"No surrendering," I said to Alcatraz. "We're going to do something *strawsome*."

Alcatraz looked at me, and he smiled.

"Drop your sword!" one of the Librarians shouted.

I held it tighter.

We'd gotten this far, and Alcatraz and I were going to find a way to get to Biblioden before he released the power of the Incarna and disintegrated everyone we knew and loved.

These Librarians weren't going to know what hit them.

17

I can't stop to write an introduction here. I'm too distracted by the multitude of puns required to do battle with a Gak. Brace yourselves, people.

The remaining Librarians closed in on us, backing us toward the edge of the platform. I grabbed Alcatraz's hand—more to keep him from getting any bright ideas about jumping off. He might be able to save us from the fall again, but I didn't want to count on it. Besides which, falling now would put us farther from Biblioden. He didn't need to kill us directly. He just needed enough time to complete his ritual and fill us all with the power of the Incarna.

"Can you break the Worldspire?" I asked Alcatraz. If

we could stop Biblioden from finishing his ritual from here, that would be even better.

Alcatraz thought about that for a moment. "It's connected to all of us, Bastille. If I break that much of it—I have no way of knowing what that might do. It might kill us. Or break the thing that connects us—our intuition, maybe? Or our ability to feel loved?"

Shattering Glass. "Don't do that, then."

The Gak still had to wind several revolutions around the tower before it would reach us.

"Drop the sword, Crystin," the head Librarian said again.

"I don't think you want me to do that!" I shouted.

The Librarians looked at each other, except for the head Librarian, who narrowed his eyes at me. "I think I very much do."

"Oh, trust me," I said. "You definitely don't."

"Why not?" the Librarian asked.

"Because my sword is connected to the tower on which we stand," I said. It wasn't, but it seemed like a plausible theory. They were both shiny, after all, and we Crystins are secretive enough about our powers that few people outside the order have any idea how they work. "One touch of my blade to the surface of the Worldspire and a great power will burst forth, which will incapacitate you all."

A few of the Librarians stepped backward, and I took the opportunity to edge closer to the staircase leading up. We needed to put some Librarians between us and the lower staircase, so that when the Gak emerged, it wasn't us it would decide to eat.

Where was Kaz when I needed him? When Alcatraz had restored the Talents, Kaz had been able to get lost and find Leavenworth, then get lost again almost immediately and find us. Given the amount of time he'd had, he couldn't have gone more than a few steps with each shift.

Find something useful, I'd told him. But he was with Leavenworth, which meant that inevitably, any useful thing they might find would arrive too late.

A tightness began to form in my chest. I didn't know if it was from the stress of waiting—patience not being my forte—or if the ritual was gathering force, the power of the Incarna starting to build up inside me and every other Free Kingdomer in the world.

"Is that so?" the head Librarian asked. He clearly didn't believe my story, which made sense—it wasn't a particularly convincing lie.

Not that I was going to admit that to him. "Yes," I said.

The head Librarian stared at me. "All right," he said. "Go ahead."

I froze.

"You don't want me to do that," I said.

The Librarian smiled. "I think I do."

I set my jaw. If I weren't such a shattering bad liar, maybe I would have gotten away with it.

Suddenly, Alcatraz held up his hands. "Step back!" he shouted. "Or I'll break you all!"

I gave Alcatraz a withering look. That wasn't how the Talents worked, and these Librarians had just had Talents of their own. He couldn't think that was going to fool them. It wasn't any better a lie than mine.

Fewer of them stepped back this time.

I heard a tapping on the steps behind us, faint at first, but growing louder. The Gak was approaching the final length of stairs.

We couldn't just stand here. I was going to have to charge. I raised my sword, ready to cut through as many of the Librarians as I could. "Alcatraz," I said, "on my go, you run for Biblioden and don't look back." I might not get to the tip of the spire to stop Biblioden, but I could make sure that Alcatraz did. He didn't think of himself as a hero, but he was. If I could only get him there, he was going to save us.

"Alcatraz! Bastille!" a voice shouted from behind the column of spire that jutted out of the center of the platform. "I lost Pop, but I hope that means I'm not arriving late!"

Just then, Kaz came ambling out. Some of the Librarians turned, and I began calculating how many of them would have to take their eyes off me before I could safely charge without leaving Alcatraz vulnerable to attack.

That alone increased my odds of cutting through their ranks. I looked to Alcatraz to give him the signal—

Shattering Glass. His eyes had an eerie sheen to them, almost like they were starting to glow.

Help was here now, but we might only have moments before it would be too late. I tightened my grip on my sword.

"Kaz!" I shouted. "We don't have much time! Please tell me you're not alone."

Kaz smiled. "What? Don't you find me useful enough, Bastille?"

I was about to shout at him that he had already *been* here, so if he was going to get lost and come back with only himself, that was a net loss, because now we were down Leavenworth.

But then I heard a sound. A sound so terrifying it cut

straight through the strange pressure now spreading in my chest. A sound much more horrifying than the slither of a Gak through an island of tall grass.

The soft yet sinister mewling of a kitten.

"Oh no," I said.

"What?" Alcatraz asked.

Not one, not two, but an entire kitten horde poured out from behind the spire after Kaz. Hundreds of kittens. Thousands of kittens. A veritable kittenpalooza, if you will.

And they weren't alone. Behind them ran Alcatraz's cousin Sing Sing Smedry, followed by Folsom Smedry, Himalaya, and their crew of reformed Librarians. My mother, sword drawn and ready for battle, took up the rear.

Himalaya wasn't dancing now. Instead, she and her company of reformed Librarians ran alongside the horde of kittens, herding them into groups. Tabbies clustered with other tabbies, calicos with calicos, black cats with white spots in one row and white cats with black spots in another. The kittens mewled their terrible mewls and bared their terrible claws, like—well, like a *kitten* you've just tried to pet because it seemed so docile and cute, but which transformed at your touch into its true form of pure, bestial, pint-sized fury and rage.

A few of the remaining Librarians screamed and

leaped from the tower to escape the oncoming horde of kittens. Others drew their swords and charged, or raised their guns and fired.

This was exactly the distraction I needed. I grabbed Alcatraz's arm. "Come on!" I shouted, and I pulled him along with me. We reached the stairs just as Biblioden's group of Librarians charged down.

Was Biblioden already finished? No. If that had happened, we'd be vapor by now. There had to be time left. There just had to be.

Across the platform, Librarians went flying as Sing, of course, tripped. I readied my sword as we reached the base of the stairs, but I needn't have. A whole regiment of tiny Persians soared overhead, claws extended. Librarians and kittens alike went flying off the side of the staircase and onto the platform below.

Alcatraz and I ducked below a volley of Siamese that followed. They rained down on the Librarians from above, teeth bared in unrestrained kitten glee. Below us, I heard my mother's battle cry as she engaged her opponents, and the screams of the Librarians as they faced the combined feline and reformed Librarian forces.

I reached the top of the stairs first, with Alcatraz right on my heels. There, standing at the spire's tip, was Biblioden.

The crow's nest around the tip of the spire was only about ten feet in diameter, so we were far too close to the Scrivener for my comfort. I expected Biblioden to turn to deal with us, but he remained focused on the spire's tip, with a single Lens held up to his eye. I could feel the power he channeled through that Lens coursing into the spire.

We had to stop him. I advanced on him with my sword raised, ready to cut the Scrivener in two.

Biblioden wasn't focusing hard enough to miss that, because he stopped, spinning around and reaching into his robes for a pair of gray Lenses.

Concussor's Lenses. He intended to knock us out so he could finish his work.

At least we'd interrupted him—although the blood-forged Lens continued to hang in the air in front of the spire's tip, glowing so bright it hurt to look at it.

"Alcatraz," I said, "can you break the Lens?"

Alcatraz focused on it, but the Lens didn't so much as crack.

And then something terrible happened. No, not to the Lens—that would have been convenient.

Biblioden started to monologue.

"You're too late," he said, putting on the Concussor's Lenses and looking at us over them. "I've finished my work. You call yourselves the Free Kingdoms, but your so-called freedom is coming to an end."

I moved to cut Biblioden down before he could finish his speech, but he raised his fingers, hovering them next to the side of his frames. "Don't come a step closer," he said, "or I'll knock you off this tower."

I lowered my sword. With my Crystin reflexes, I could reach an average Librarian before he knocked me out with a beam of light. I could even do so with an *above-average* Librarian without breaking a sweat.

But this was Biblioden the Scrivener. I couldn't count on my ability to best him with brute force.

So, instead of edging toward him, I began to edge toward Alcatraz.

"Why are you doing this?" Alcatraz asked. "You've got all of the Hushlands under your control. Isn't that good enough for you?"

I inched closer. Alcatraz had the Slantviewer's Lenses tucked into his jacket pocket. I kept my sword low, trying not to appear like a threat.

Which, being me, is practically impossible, I'll have you know.

"You Smedrys sow disorder," Biblioden said. "Do you think I don't know what your father was planning? He wanted to give Smedry Talents to *everyone* in the *world*! Think of what a disaster that would be! No, you Smedrys have never been satisfied with the Free Kingdoms. You have to scatter your chaos. If it isn't destroyed, it will spread everywhere. We tried for years to conquer you, but now we're going to do much better. It'll be like you never existed at all!"

That was such a long monologue that I'd managed to get myself right next to Alcatraz in slow enough increments that Biblioden didn't seem to have noticed. I eased my hand over to Alcatraz's pocket and slowly withdrew the Slantviewer's Lenses.

Biblioden's eyes flicked to me, only for a second, before Alcatraz shouted at him, "You're going to pay for what you did to my father!"

(Yes, Alcatraz did realize what I was doing. Yes, he was intentionally trying to help me. Yes, I know this because I asked him.)

Biblioden smiled. "Your father deserved what he got," he said. "And so do you, and the rest of the Smedrys. In fact—"

I don't know what Biblioden was going to say next, because the Slantviewer's Lenses began to glow in my hand, and I shoved them hastily onto my face, setting Biblioden as the target, and then myself. That got Biblioden's attention. I didn't even have to raise my sword before he blasted me with his Concussor's Lenses.

I felt the power of the blast as it passed through me. The Lenses were hot on my face, and for a moment they felt like an extension of my body, powerful and alive. Like with Etna, the blast transferred through me,

knocking Biblioden back against the railing of the crow's nest, stunned and blinking and holding his head.

I told you earlier that I am not an Oculator. But for that one moment, I basically was.

How did it feel, you ask?

It felt *AWESOME*.

Biblioden lay in the crow's nest, fallen but not entirely beaten. I was about to raise my sword and finish the job when—

"Gak!" a Librarian shouted from below us, and I looked out over the railing to see the Gak—looking somewhat winded after its long trek up the tower—finally cresting the top of the stairs. The Librarian troops parted, and the kitten regiments wasted no time, pouncing upon the fleeing Librarians, teeth and claws bloody and bared. Even the people on our side scattered, many of them cowering behind my mother, who stood guard in front of them at one edge of the platform.

The Gak met my eyes and exposed its terrible teeth in a wide and threatening grin.

"Shattering Glass," I said. "It came all the way over here for *us*."

Now, if I were a Gak, I would no doubt also have wanted revenge on the people who stabbed me, escaped from my island—thus depriving me of a meal—and then broke gravity and abandoned me in the ocean. Still, I had expected it to be distracted by the many potential meals presenting themselves on the platform below, but no. It turns out Gaks have priorities.

The Gak slithered directly toward us.

We had a few moments before it reached us. I grabbed Alcatraz by the arm and skirted the edge of the crow's nest, putting Biblioden between us and the top of the pinnacle stairs. It didn't help though. The Gak ignored the stairs entirely and began to coil around the stalk of the spire, slithering up toward us. My mother drew her sword and slashed toward the Gak, but was intercepted by the cultish Librarians, who tumbled down on top of my mother in their efforts to get away from the Gak.

Biblioden hardly seemed to notice. He remained where he had fallen, the power that gushed through his Lens increasing.

If a *Gak* wouldn't distract him, I wasn't sure what would. I didn't have time to ponder it, because at that moment the Gak's toothy face appeared over the edge of the crow's nest, right by my hip.

"Well, well," the Gak said. "Nice to see you again."

"This does feel strawdly familiar," Alcatraz said.

"Alcatraz," I said, "I don't think that's going to help this time."

"Fine," Alcatraz said, "I withstraw the comment."

The Gak chortled menacingly. "I knew you might have some extraw ideas for me," the Gak said. "But I won't be distrawcted this time."

"I forestraw that this might be the case," I said. By the Sands, this wasn't helping. All we were doing was putting off our inevitable demise at the hands of the Gak in favor of our inevitable vaporization at the hands of Biblioden. There had to be something else we could do. I still had my sword, but I wasn't going to beat the Gak with that. I could swing for Biblioden, but the Gak's body snaked in between us, blocking me from attacking him. I looked to Alcatraz. "Don't you have any brilliant ideas?"

Alcatraz shrugged. "I think my accounts are overstrawn."

"That one's a stretch," the Gak said. "I think we're finished now."

Its neck wrapped around us, nudging Alcatraz's knees to draw us closer together. Shattering Glass, it was going to eat us both at once. To Alcatraz's credit, at least this time he wasn't whining about it, but—

Oh. *Oh!* I had an idea.

"You touched him!" I said to the Gak. "You touched Alcatraz, and now you owe me a service."

"I'm afraid that's not how it works," the Gak said. "I only owe you a service if I touch straw, and I didn't—"

"He's a straw man!" I shouted. "Alcatraz is a straw man! A person lacking in substance and integrity! Just ask him!"

The Gak turned to Alcatraz, raising one of its crooked eyebrows. "Is that so?" it asked.

Alcatraz nodded. "Oh, yeah. I'm the worst."

I grinned. For once, I couldn't be more pleased that he thought so.

The Gak sighed, and perhaps because it had far more meal options available on this tower than it did on the island, it relented. "Fine," it said to me. "I owe you a service. I suppose you want me not to eat you."

"No," I said, and I pointed right at Biblioden. "I want you to eat *him*."

The Gak grinned and slithered over toward the other side of the platform. *That* finally caught Biblioden's attention. The power at the tip of the spire was growing strong enough to make my ears pop.

I wish I had a picture of Biblioden's face as the Gak advanced on him. It would have been even better than the picture of Alcatraz wearing a tunic. Biblioden scrambled back, and then seemed to realize that if he took one more step, he was going to drop into a mess of kittens and reformed Librarians. The Gak slithered upward so the front half of its bulbous body coiled around the tip of the spire, looming over Biblioden.

"Wait!" Biblioden shouted. "Straw down! Straw you later! I'm too young to straw! By the Sands, why is it so difficult to think of words that sound like—"

Biblioden didn't get to finish that sentence, because the Gak unhinged its irregular jaw, revealing jagged teeth extending down its throat in orderly, vibrating rows. I'm not sure how much integrity Biblioden had, but he definitely had a lot of substance, all of which was now in the mouth of the Gak.

My editor won't let me tell you what exactly the Gak did to Biblioden, but I can tell you this: faster than you can say "Chihuahuas, cheese, and crackers," the remaining Librarians who witnessed it scattered.

When it finished, the Gak turned on us again. "Any reason I shouldn't eat you two for dessert?"

The pressure in my chest hadn't lessened, and it was beginning to travel down my arms in tingles, like my limbs were slowly falling asleep. Maybe that was the power being released. Maybe it was dissipating, traveling down my fingers, getting ready to leave my body.

"Yes," I said. "That guy you ate was preparing to unleash magical energy that will course through the bodies of all Free Kingdomers, and we're the only ones who can stop it. You don't want to eat us before we do that."

"That would be strawgonizing," Alcatraz supplied.

I gave Alcatraz a side-eye, and he shrugged. "I'm getting to the bottom of the hay bale, here."

"It would indeed," the Gak said. "I like you two. I want you to live to be eaten another day. Besides, ancient Librarians are difficult to digest. I'll take my leave for now."

And with that, the Gak slithered off the spire tip and down the stairs leading back to the ocean.

Alcatraz turned to me and grinned. "A straw man. That was amazing, Bastille."

"Eh," I said. "It was all your sulking that gave me the idea. Told you you were a hero."

Alcatraz smiled, though when he looked at me it quickly faded. "Bastille," he said, "your eyes are glowing."

I nodded. "Yours too." The pressure in my chest continued to build, until it felt like my body might burst.

Alcatraz stared at the tip of the Worldspire, his eyes

now definitely glowing with an eerie light. "It's already happening," he said. "The energy is filling the people of the Free Kingdoms. I don't know how to stop it." He looked down at the pale glowing light emanating from the base of his fingernails. My own were doing the same.

I peered over the edge of the crow's nest. Below us, the reformed Librarians were now glowing, though—with the help of Kaz—they were getting the upper hand. Folsom had used some of the rope to tie up a number of Librarians, while others lay prone, pinned beneath tidy piles of Russian Blues and Canadian Sphynxes. The horrible mewling continued, and my skin crawled, not only from the terror of the sight, but also from the knowledge that at any moment we could all be vaporized, and the kittens would be the only ones left with the evil Librarians.

I didn't know how long we had, but unless one of us could do something, all of us Free Kingdomers— Smedrys included—were about to discorporate, burning up like the entire Incarna civilization.

My mother looked up and met my eyes. There was a question in her expression, and from the way her face fell when she saw me, I could tell she knew the answer just by looking at me.

We were too late after all.

Chapter

18

This seems like a good time to talk about endings. As a reader of fiction, you've read many of them. You know what to expect. The characters in books always *think* they've failed right before they ultimately succeed. This is why many of you felt betrayed at the end of the fifth volume of this story—Alcatraz wasn't *supposed* to fail. He was *supposed* to win.

I feel that I need to remind you Hushlanders that this is not a work of fiction. It is a completely true account of what happened that day at the top of the Worldspire. I am not manipulating the events to give you a satisfying conclusion—at this point in our story, Alcatraz and I really were standing on top of the Worldspire thinking that we'd failed. We'd been too late. We hadn't saved the

Free Kingdoms. We were merely standing at the very center of the world at the time of their demise.

I point this out because I want you to remember it as you read. I can't change what happened simply to satisfy your need for a happy ending.

Which makes what happened next all the more exciting, if you ask me.

I turned around and reached for Alcatraz's hand— this time for comfort.

And as I did, the light of the sun caught on a bit of glass at the center of the platform, resting against the final stretch of spire.

The bloodforged Lens. A slim circle of glass without a frame or a rim. As I bent down to pick it up, the Lens had a *feeling* about it—deep and dark and terrible, even though it was only a piece of glass.

Alcatraz? a voice said in my head. *Is that you?*

I froze. I could have sworn—

Alcatraz? the voice said again. *I knew you'd make it. I knew you'd be able to save us.*

I *recognized* that voice.

"Alcatraz," I said.

No, I'm not Alcatraz, Attica said in my mind. *He escaped. They sacrificed me instead.*

"Alcatraz," I said again, ignoring the increasing

protests from the Lens. "I think . . . I think I found your father."

Alcatraz's face darkened, which is an odd expression to use for something that was literally glowing, more and more every second. "What do you mean you found him? He's not lost. He's—"

Who is this? Attica asked from the Lens. *Of course you've found me. Where else would I be?*

Where else would he be? Dead. That's where we all thought he was, anyway.

"Attica, it's Bastille," I said. Alcatraz's eyes widened, and he stared at the Lens in my hand.

Bastille! Attica said in my head. *Wonderful. Alcatraz can't be far behind.*

I should have been pleased with Attica's faith in me, but in truth I wanted to shake him. And since I was holding a Lens apparently containing his consciousness, I did.

"What are you doing?" Alcatraz asked.

Is he nearby? Attica asked. *Quickly. We don't have much time.*

Apparently Attica's sense of equilibrium hadn't transferred to the Lens. Didn't mean I wouldn't shake him to my heart's content when we all got ourselves out of this.

What was he doing in the Lens? What on earth had that Smedry done now?

"Your father isn't dead," I said. "He's in here." I shoved the bloodforged Lens into Alcatraz's hands, holding on so I'd continue to be able to hear Attica.

The Lens didn't activate, not immediately. But I could feel power humming through it, passing between Alcatraz and me. The power of the Incarna, about to destroy us.

"Dad?" Alcatraz asked.

Alcatraz, there you are! Attica said. *I knew you'd make it in time. Everything is going exactly according to plan.*

Shattering Smedrys. "That is not possible," I said. "Because you are in a bloodforged Lens, and we're all starting to glow and are about to explode."

Not at all! Attica said. *You're about to be vaporized! Exactly as I'd hoped.*

"Um, Dad?" Alcatraz said. "Even I know that's a terrible plan."

Of course it is, Attica said. *Which is why you need to act while there's still time. The channel is open and the power is flowing, but we have a few minutes yet before it kills anyone.*

"Okay," Alcatraz said. "How do we turn it off?"

You can't, Attica said, as if this were the most obvious thing in the world.

I wanted to hit him. I wanted to throw the bloodforged Lens on the ground and crunch it under my heel. "If we can't," I said through my teeth, "then what does it matter if it takes a few minutes?"

Tears were starting to run down Alcatraz's face again. "I'm sorry, Dad," he said. "I'm sorry I let them sacrifice you."

Nonsense, Attica said. *As I said, it's all happening exactly as I hoped.*

"You *planned* for them to sacrifice you?" I asked. "That is the worst plan I've ever heard, and I spend my life protecting Smedrys!"

The power of the Incarna, Attica said. *Our family has been bearing it for years. It needs to be released. Someone had to go into this Lens so that we could open the way. I'm sorry you had to see that, Alcatraz, but it had to be done.*

"What good does it do to release it if it's going to *kill us all*?" I asked. Attica didn't make any more shattering sense in death than he did in life, and I had half a mind to snap his Lens in two and see if that would stop the power.

But if it didn't, we'd be down one Lens, and possibly one more Smedry who could have helped us stop it. If he ever managed to get to the point.

The power is too great a burden for any one group of

people to bear, Attica said. *It needs to be given to everyone. Every person in the world must have access to it.*

After dealing with an army of Talented Librarians, that sounded like yet another way to end the world.

"We can't give them all Talents, Dad," Alcatraz said. "That would be chaos."

The power will be diluted for everyone else, Attica said. *It won't be enough to kill anyone, or to burst forth and cause destruction. Everyone will have a Talent, but only a small one. A habit of losing their keys perhaps, or an inability to step over obstacles without stubbing their toe. I knew this was going to happen, and so I positioned myself here. Together, we can release the power of the Incarna and share the burden with the world, Hushlands and Free Kingdoms alike.*

And then, Alcatraz, you can figure out how to get me out of this Lens.

I wasn't sure I believed that Attica had *meant* to get turned into a bloodforged Lens. More likely he was just claiming that he'd had that kind of foresight, now that it had worked out the way he'd always wanted.

But Attica announcing that he expected Alcatraz to get him out of the Lens . . . Alcatraz had yanked his father free from the clutches of the Curators of Alexandria once, but this—

"I don't think we're going to be able to free him, Alcatraz," I said. "And I don't think it's fair of him to expect that you'll be able to do that."

Alcatraz sniffed once, and then nodded. "I'm going to try," he said. "But first, Dad, tell me how to redirect the power."

I assume you do it with this Lens, Attica said. *But that's all the guidance I can give you.*

Of course it was. I let go of the Lens and stomped my foot on the crystal platform. "This isn't fair to you," I said. "He can't simply expect you to know how to save the world after he got himself into this fix. It's not—"

"Bastille," Alcatraz said, "do you think I can do this?"

Alcatraz watched me like he cared what my answer was, like he was asking my honest opinion.

At that moment, I was an Oculator. I could have insisted that Alcatraz let *me* try.

But Alcatraz was *amazing.* I'd seen him do so many impossible things, I'd lost count.

Alcatraz needed to finish his father's work, however misguided that work might have been. This was his moment. His turn to be a hero.

"Yes," I said. "Do it. Save us. I know you can."

Alcatraz smiled at me, his eyes now glowing bright enough to read by. I lifted the Slantviewer's Lenses back to my eyes. They immediately began to heat up and I put them on quickly, targeting first Alcatraz and then the spire.

I watched as Alcatraz raised the Lens to his eye. I could see the torrents of power coursing through the spire, funneled through the bloodforged Lens. That was what it did—it *handled* the power of the Incarna, directing it. The power was like a living thing, or maybe it merely flowed *through* every living thing, a great force of immeasurable power that connected all of us.

Alcatraz had spent his whole life fighting the splinter of that power that made its way through him. He'd fought with it, grown with it, *understood* it in ways few people ever would. I saw the power through Alcatraz's perspective, and I could see the pattern of it, the ways it built and flowed, swelled and ebbed. Through his eyes, it felt *familiar* to me. Comprehensible. Clear.

Alcatraz channeled his own power through the Lens, and I saw what he was doing. He was breaking us all, just a little, enough that the power could flow through the cracks in us and escape.

There was a great shattering sound, as if the Worldspire was breaking apart, although nothing moved. My skin broke out in goosebumps, and then the pressure in my chest began to lessen, like a deflating balloon. My

Lenses stopped working, and I shoved them in my pocket. My fingernails faded to normal; Alcatraz's eyes ceased to glow. From down below, I heard Kaz give a great whoop, and then the rest of our friends erupted in cheers. The other Smedrys—probably all Free Kingdomers—could feel it. We'd done it. We'd saved them.

Alcatraz shoved the Lens in his pocket, then looked at me.

"We did it," I said. "We saved the Free Kingdoms. You saved us. And in my book, that makes you a hero."

Alcatraz's face crumpled, and he stumbled forward. I barely caught him before he collapsed right into the tip of the spire.

And then I held him while he cried.

Chapter
• 19 •

I mentioned in Chapter Seventeen that patience wasn't my forte. That was a lie, sparked by the stress of the situation.

I'll have you know I'm quite patient.

Don't believe me?

Consider for a moment all the things I was not doing while I was standing on the top of the Worldspire next to Alcatraz.

I was not stealing the bloodforged Lens from Alcatraz so I could chew out his father for everything he continued to put Alcatraz through.

I was not railing against fate for standing me at a dizzying height with my only other option being to descend into a collective of bloodthirsty kittens.

And when an airship neared the spire, and I saw Alcatraz's mother, Shasta Smedry (who had apparently escaped from the Librarians on the ship), looking out from the front, I didn't even curse at her for showing up only after everything was over, or for showing up at all.

Much, anyway.

"Why does your mother always appear at the most inconvenient times?" I asked Alcatraz.

"I don't know," he said. "If I didn't know better, I'd think it was her Talent."

Shasta had the same Talent as Attica—the ability to lose things. She was also a Librarian. I supposed I should be grateful she arrived at the end of the battle. Her presence would only have complicated things.

I still thought Alcatraz should have at least one parent who supported him. But he had the rest of us, which I supposed would have to suffice.

A ramp descended from the airship to the platform below us, and Shasta stepped onto it. The reformed Librarians were sorting the remainder of the kittens into organized groups, though the mewling was growing louder now that they didn't have evil Librarians on whom to exact their bloody feline vengeance.

Alcatraz and I hurried down the staircase to meet

her, joined by Sing and Kaz. My mother stood in front, ready to defend us from Shasta if required.

Draulin did look somewhat relieved to see me all in one piece, and I had to admit I felt the same about her.

Shasta opened her mouth to speak, but was cut off by a loud voice rounding the spire behind us. "Hastening Howes, boy!" Leavenworth called. "What did I miss?"

Kaz turned around and beckoned for his father to join us. "Alcatraz saved us," he said. "I think. You did save us, didn't you, Alcatraz?"

Alcatraz smiled and elbowed me. "Bastille did a lot of it," he said.

I blushed. Daintily.

"All right," Shasta said. "Now that we have that out of the way, maybe you'll explain what happened."

Alcatraz pulled the Lens out of his pocket. "Biblioden tried to channel the power of the Incarna to kill everyone in the Free Kingdoms." He held up the Lens. "Using this."

"The bloodforged Lens," Leavenworth said grimly. "The one they killed Attica to make."

Shasta didn't look particularly surprised at the news of Attica's death, so I took it she'd already heard.

"He's not dead," Alcatraz said. "Not completely. He's inside the Lens. Or his soul is, maybe. We spoke to him."

That did seem to surprise her. "Give it to me."

Alcatraz hesitated. Even if she was his mother, he wasn't going to hand over a bloodforged Lens to a Librarian.

Leavenworth held out his hand. "I'll take it, my boy," he said.

Alcatraz paused another moment, then handed over the Lens. Leavenworth closed his eyes, most likely hearing Attica's voice for himself.

"Oh, Attica," Leavenworth said. "None of us could have known what was going to happen. Not even you."

I was pretty sure Leavenworth was right.

"Attica got what he wanted," I told the others. "There's a little bit of Smedry Talent in every person in the world now."

Shasta looked a bit stunned, no doubt thinking of the inevitable chaos that would cause, even if they weren't top-tier Talents.

Though really, who knew? There might be someone out there—several someones, even—discovering an odd ability to break everything they touched at that very moment. Some of them might wonder if they were prone to destruction.

I suppose, dear reader, that it might even be you.

"If that's the case," Shasta said, "our work will be more important than ever." She seemed to be speaking mostly to Himalaya and the group of reformed Librarians, some of whom nodded. "The Librarians are in need of leadership," Shasta continued. "I intend to provide that leadership. We can change things from within."

"Keep the Hushlanders in the dark, you mean," Alcatraz said.

Shasta looked at him. "There will be enough chaos, enough change, resulting from today's events. Someday perhaps we can show them the truth, but we can't do everything all at once."

I had strong doubts that Shasta ever intended to free the Hushlanders from Librarian lies. But she also wasn't Biblioden. And she'd helped us on a number of occasions.

"We need to end the war," Kaz said. "That's the most important thing."

Shasta nodded. "That's exactly what I intend to do."

"I'm all for it," Himalaya said. "And Kaz found us a whole lot of kittens while we were lost, and I think they want to help."

I shuddered at the sort of "help" they were likely to provide.

Shasta pressed her thin lips together, looking at Alcatraz over the tops of her horn-rimmed glasses. "You can come with me."

Alcatraz shook his head. "I don't belong in the Hush-lands," he said. "I never did."

I reached for his hand again. That was true. He was a Smedry. He belonged with his family. Shasta was his mother, but she'd lost her relationship with her son. Attica had lost his humanity. Maybe these were manifestations of their Talents, or maybe they were just people who made terrible mistakes.

Alcatraz, though, still had a family. He had Leavenworth, and Kaz, and all the Smedry cousins. Family bonds that—despite his Talent—could never be broken.

"I'll be in touch," Shasta said. And she began instructing the reformed Librarians to load their army of kittens into the airship.

I was sure *that* was going to go well.

While Kaz and Leavenworth were seeing Folsom off—he and Himalaya were going with Shasta and the reformed Librarians—my mother approached, apparently satisfied that no one needed defending from Shasta at the moment. Draulin wore her customary glower, and I braced for her inevitable chastisement for all the reckless, Smedry-like things I had done.

Instead, she did something surprising.

She hugged me.

"Gak!" I said.

"I'm sorry I dragged you into this," my mother said. "You've done well. You've done *very* well, Bastille. Despite my unwelcome interference at times."

"Uh . . ."

Okay, so *this* was weird. I mean, I love my mother and all, but she's normally about as affectionate as a dead llama. There was no escaping from this hug though—my mother has always been quite a good grappler.

And remarkably, I didn't want to escape. It may have made me feel better, a little.

Don't tell my mother I said that.

When I finally extracted myself, Alcatraz and I sat on the steps leading up to the tip of the Worldspire.

Alcatraz crossed his arms, a defeated look on his face. We'd won, but at a high cost, especially for him. I wished I could have prevented him from seeing the horrible things he'd seen, and losing the people he'd lost.

"It's still not your fault, you know," I said.

Alcatraz shrugged. "It's not yours either."

"I know," I said. I'd done my best to protect the Smedrys, but they kept getting in trouble, because that's what Smedrys do.

I hated that Alcatraz still bore the weight of everything on his shoulders. He too had done the best he could.

Then I had an idea. "I still have the Slantviewer's Lenses," I said, pulling them out of a pocket in my armor.

"Oh," Alcatraz said. "But you can't use them anymore, can you?"

The Lenses stayed cold and inert in my hand. "No," I said. I felt a bit wistful about that, but honestly, I had thought I'd *never* know what it felt like to be an Oculator. The fact that I got that experience, if only for a moment, made me feel, well . . .

Lucky.

I handed the Lenses to Alcatraz. "Maybe you should see what your grandfather thinks about you. Once and

for all." I gestured toward Leavenworth, helping Himalaya wrangle the last of the kittens.

Alcatraz hesitated. Then he looked at his grandfather and activated the Lenses, and looked down at his
own reflection in the crystal spire and activated them
again.

Grandpa Smedry looked up just then, and spotted
Alcatraz with the Lenses. He smiled.

Alcatraz's shoulders drooped, and he pressed his lips
together. His eyes filled with tears behind the Lenses.
"That's not who I am," Alcatraz said.

From the look on his face, I knew the old Smedry felt
otherwise.

"Maybe not," I said. "But the coward who destroys
things—that isn't who you are either."

Alcatraz reached up and deactivated the Lenses, and
then he looked at me. Our eyes met for a split second,
and he touched the Lenses again, then looked at his own
reflection and reactivated them.

Alcatraz blushed. Then I blushed. And then he blushed
some more. Alcatraz took off the Slantviewer's Lenses
and shoved them in his pocket.

Then he took my hand. We sat in silence for a
moment.

This is how patient I am: I didn't even punch him.

"All right," Kaz said, after the airship of Librarians had left us. "Ready to get lost?"

"Ready as I'll ever be," Alcatraz said.

I stood up. "Ready for anything," I told him. Then we followed Kaz down to the bottom of the spire, and off to our next adventure.

EPILOGUE

It took several years before Alcatraz and I got married. (What? We were kids when all of this happened. Of course it took several years.) Our wedding took place in the castle at Nalhalla, and more or less the entire city came out to celebrate. (Even the dragons, who customarily celebrate by munching on maidens, but in this case were limited to large sections of wedding cake. It's a good thing some Smedrys are so bad at math or there would never have been enough to go around.) Afterward— while Folsom and Himalaya led a conga line around the courtyard that threatened to knock over every table it passed—I found Alcatraz standing on a balcony overlooking the party.

He smiled as I approached. My dress made a soft tinkling sound as I walked, so a wedding-day ninja I was not. (My father had the whole thing commissioned out of Glassweave, so it didn't matter if my enemies heard me coming.) There was something sad in his expression, which isn't exactly what a girl wants to see from her brand-new husband on her wedding day.

But I could think of a number of reasons for it that had nothing to do with me.

"Seen any hint of your Talent yet?" Alcatraz asked.

"Not yet," I told him. The Smedrys, as it turned out, had retained their regular-force Talents, even as the rest of the world acquired smaller ones. "If it breaks my dress, I'm going to stab it."

"I don't think that's how it works, Bastille."

"A girl can dream," I said. "How did it go with your mother?" Shasta was the last person I'd seen Alcatraz with, so she was my first guess as to the source of his sadness. Though things seemed to have been going better with her lately. She at least appeared to be holding up her end of the deal, reforming the Librarians.

"Yeah," Alcatraz said. "It went fine."

"And your father?"

"In his Lens stand at the head table," Alcatraz said. "He seemed happy about it."

"Then why are you hiding up here by yourself?" I asked.

Alcatraz winced. "I got cornered by Mr. Bagsworth from the publishing company again."

Oh. Alcatraz had spent the last few years writing the first five volumes of his autobiography, which had been a massive success in the Free Kingdoms, and even gained a small but tenacious audience in the Hushlands. He'd just completed the fifth volume, but had been avoiding turning it in. I knew he felt bad for letting everyone down by not producing a more satisfying end to the story, but he swore—no matter how much I tried to convince him otherwise—that he wouldn't be able to adequately write about the events leading up to the Worldspire.

Below us, the conga line of Librarians and Smedrys grew longer, and then shorter again when the back half of the line—beginning with Kaz—got lost just enough to snake around the courtyard in an entirely different direction.

"I know you think I should continue the story, Bastille," Alcatraz said miserably. "But I can't. That part of the story—it's too painful. I can't relive it."

"I know," I said. "That's why I've decided to write it for you."

Alcatraz turned to stare at me. "What?"

"Turn in the fifth book the way you've written it," I told him, "and I'll write the rest for you." I'd had this idea for a while now, but I'd hoped that Al would find it in himself to finish the story on his own. "I was there for everything left that needs to be written, and I probably remember it better than you do."

"Yes, but . . ." Alcatraz hesitated. "You really think you're up to . . ."

"Remembering what an idiot you were?" I asked. "I think I can handle it."

"Writing a book?"

I turned toward him, resting my hip against the railing of the balcony. "What is that supposed to mean? Of course I'm up to writing a book. I'm *literate*. And I'm sure I can get one of those literary licenses somewhere."

Alcatraz smiled. "You'd do that for me?"

"Of course," I told him. "That's what people who love you are here for." Alcatraz reached over to put his hand on top of mine.

"Also for punching you when you need it," I added.

"Bastille," Alcatraz said.

"And for yelling true things at you when you most need to hear them," I said.

"Bastille?"

"And for dragging you along by your ear when you're

too depressed to know that you ought to be saving the world, and—"

"Bastille!" Alcatraz said, and then he gripped my hand hard and pulled me away from the edge of the balcony.

Right before the railing crumbled into pieces and went tumbling down into the courtyard below.

I blinked at it. "Please tell me you did that," I said.

"No," Alcatraz said. "I think it's safe to say that one was you."

I was pretty sure we were going to be having that argument daily for the rest of our lives.

So this one time, I let Alcatraz think he was right.

Bastille's Afterword

And so we come to the end of our story. This is the part where I'm supposed to tell you to make up your own mind about Alcatraz, but I'm not that generous.

Alcatraz is a hero. If you say otherwise, I will stab you.

(Just ask Alcatraz. You cannot imagine how many puncture wounds the man has had to endure.)

Alcatraz insists to this day that he isn't a hero (despite frequent stabbings), not only because he is stoopid, but because—as you've probably noticed—we may have saved the world, but we also failed in several large and important ways.

We never did find a way to get Attica out of the Lens. And he and Alcatraz never truly came to understand each other. Al's relationship with his mother didn't fare much better, nor did my relationship with mine. And that bullet is going to catch up to Leavenworth eventually.

As Alcatraz would say, some things, once broken, can't ever be fixed.

What I hope you learn is that heroes aren't perfect people. We aren't all-powerful beings with absolute control. We are deeply flawed. We make mistakes, we act rashly, and sometimes we fail.

Heroes, I think, are the people who get up and try anyway, even when we know the odds are stacked against us. Even when the world is broken beyond repair. We do our best to protect others, to keep bad things from happening, and to stand up to people who cause destruction and pain—even when we don't entirely succeed at it.

And then afterward, we live with the consequences. Which may be the hardest part of all.

You're welcome.

Bastille Smedry

Alcatraz's Afterword

This is me. Alcatraz.

Yes, I know I said I was done. I said no more writing. I said the fifth book was the last book.

I lied. It turns out that Bastille Smedry is even more of a bully than I'd anticipated. And . . . well, maybe she's also wiser than I give her credit for.

Most of the events she wrote about in this book are true. (Though I'm not thrilled with her commentary.) The emotion, though . . . I don't know if she nailed that. It would be difficult for anyone—myself included—to express just how painful it still feels to have abandoned my father to the enemy. Yes, everyone else can applaud the fact that ultimately, I didn't let Biblioden destroy the world. But I was still a coward during a very critical moment of my life.

Now that this volume is complete, perhaps I can finally explain exactly why I'm no hero. My job was to protect you from the Librarians. And yet in the end, I let them touch your soul and alter it. Worse, my only option was to go further and give each and every one of you a little sliver of Smedry Talent.

It's there inside of you, and always has been. You've probably dismissed it. The stubborn hair that simply won't behave. Or perhaps electronics work differently for you than they do for others. Or maybe you can't step over anything without stubbing your toe. Or it's your ability to lose things in your own pockets, only to have them re-appear later on.

Or an inexplicable ability to break things without trying.

My burden has become yours. In the end, my father got what he wanted, if not on the scale he intended. In acknowledging this, I guess I'm admitting the real (actual, final) reason I wrote this autobiography. It's a guidebook.

So try, if you can, to remember the things I've learned. The seed of the Talent is inside you, and at times it's going to come out and ruin things. But it's also part of what makes you special.

I'm not always a good person. But I'm not *just* a coward either. Sometimes I'm heroic. Sometimes I'm selfish. I'm all those things at once.

I'm...well, I'm a human being. Like you. I often make mistakes, and sometimes I repeat them. But maybe... maybe there is one thing I've finally learned.

Sometimes the curse you see as your biggest flaw can somehow also be your greatest advantage.

And sometimes you need your friends to help you see that.

Alcatraz Smedry

THE END
(Yes, the real one.)

and then I was vaporized, reduced to a gaseous con-
glomeration of floating elements that were once Bastille.
"Alcatraz, you idiot," I said, "this ending is even worse
than the last one."

"You can't tell me that," Alcatraz said. "Gaseous clouds
don't have mouths."

"And yet somehow you keep talking," I said, and then
I stopped, because I realized he was right.

THE END

ABOUT THE AUTHORS

Brandon Sanderson is the fake author of these books, the name Alcatraz publishes them under to keep the Librarians from realizing that the books are real. Alcatraz has it on good authority that while there was once an actual Brandon Sanderson, he was executed for taking too much time to write the fifth book of a series—and then doing something horrible at the ending. These days, the title "Brandon Sanderson" is wielded by a group of shadowy book-writing ninjas, with the goal of owning all of the world's mac and cheese.

Janci Patterson is the pen name of Bastille Smedry. The real Janci Patterson writes romance novels—the most outlandish kind of fantasy—which are dictated to her by her army of twelve-inch plastic dolls.

ABOUT THE ILLUSTRATOR

Hayley Lazo may not be a Librarian Spy, but her obsession with grammar, fleet of adopted whale sharks, and extraterrestrial origins uncovered by Free Kingdoms agents leave room for concern. Her art can be found at studiozealot.com. Approach with caution and shark treats.

ACKNOWLEDGMENTS

As a longtime Alcatraz fan, I am so grateful to have been a part of the completion of this series. Working on this book was pure joy from start to finish, and I am forever thankful to Brandon for letting me be a part of it. Special thanks to Emily Sanderson for believing in me and my work, and for suggesting I might be a good fit for the project. It's been an honor to work in this world, and with both of you.

I'm also thankful to all my early readers, including Megan Walker and my writing group, the often-renamed Seizure Ninjas. Special thanks to Cortana Olds, who was the first person ever to read through *The Dark Talent* and immediately begin this volume. Cortana has read the series dozens of times, remembers it better than I do, and was always willing to explain to me where exactly I would find this event or that joke. Thanks always to my husband, Drew Olds, for laughing at my jokes, for believing in me and my work, and for always being available when I just need someone to read a scene and tell me it's good.

· Acknowledgments ·

Thanks to the Dragonsteel team, who are amazing at their jobs. Isaac Stewart helped with the plot development, and especially with the ending. Thank you, Isaac, for the ideas, for the support, and as always, for your friendship. Isaac also directed the art, and he and Hayley Lazo did an amazing job bringing Bastille's story to life—and many thanks to Anna Early, who assisted Hayley on a few final illustrations in order to meet tight deadlines. Karen Ahlstrom's continuity documents were a lifesaver while writing this book, and she gave excellent feedback on the finished draft. Kristina Kugler squeezed in a line edit for me on short notice, and her editing made this book much, much better than it was. Thank you, Kristy, for always supporting me and my work, and for making my sentences infinitely more readable. Peter Ahlstrom is an incredible editor, and I'm so grateful for his dedication to making all of Brandon's books the best they can be.

Special thanks are due to the Dragonsteel beta team—you guys are incredible, and I'm so thankful for the privilege of working with you. Betas for this book included Darci Cole, Paige Vest, Jennifer Neal, Becca Reppert, Richard Fife, Deana Covel Whitney, Alice Arneson, Linnea Lindstrom, Kalyani Poluri, Zaya Clinger, and Alexander Whitney. Your feedback helped shape this book into a better version of itself, and your friendship made the process more wonderful as well. Gamma readers included several of the above, plus Brian T. Hill, Chris McGrath, Joy Allen, Eliyahu Berelowitz Levin, Jessica Ashcraft, Brandon Cole, Ari Kufer, Ian McNatt, Ted Herman, Bob Kluttz, Aaron Biggs, Sam Baskin, Taylor Cole, Gary Singer, Glen Vogelaar, Alexis Horizon, Ross Newberry, Tim Challener, Heather Clinger, Dr. Kathleen Holland, Rebecca Arneson, Rahul Pantula, Evgeni "Argent" Kirilov, Eric Lake, Chana Oshira Block, and Aaron Ford.

Thanks to the team at Tor, including Susan Chang and Rachel Bass, for shepherding this book through its development. Susan's notes were instrumental in shaping the book from an early draft into the version you see now, and I'm grateful for her insight and her love of the series.

Thanks also to my agent, Eddie Schneider, and the whole team at JABberwocky, for looking out for me and for putting out so many fires. My job would be much, much harder without you.

And thanks most of all to you, our readers. Thank you for giving this book a chance, even after a very long wait. I hope you love it, and I hope my additions to the series have done justice to the stories you love.

Janci Patterson